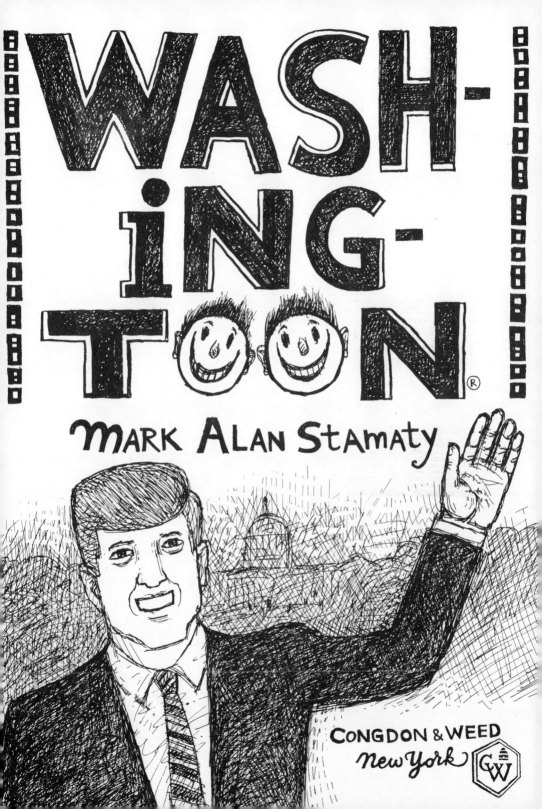

Copyright © 1983 by Mark Alan Stamaty

Library of Congress Catalog Card Number: 83-71709

ISBN 0-86553-097-1

ISBN 0-312-92925-0 (St. Martin's Press)

Published by CONGDON & WEED, INC.
298 Fifth Avenue, New York, N.Y. 10001

Distributed by St. Martin's Press
175 Fifth Avenue, New York, N.Y. 10010

Published simultaneously in Canada by
METHUEN PUBLICATIONS
2330 Midland Avenue
AGINCOURT, ONTARIO M1S 1P7

This BOOK is DEDICATED
to:

DAVID SCHNEIDERMAN
and
MEG GREENFIELD

ACKNOWLEDGEMENTS:

Thank you to ALL tHE KiND and PATiENT PEOPLE WHO ALLOWED me to PiCK tHEiR BRAiNS unmercifully AS PART OF my EFFORT to EDUCATE MYSELF ABOUt WASHiNGTON.

m. a. s.

MARCH 3RD, 1977. 2:14 A.M.

NOT AGAIN.

YOUR NERVES, GERRY?

YES, DAMMIT. I HAVEN'T HAD A GOOD NIGHT'S SLEEP SINCE THEY BLOCKED THAT MERGER.

WEARILY, GERARD V. OXBOGGLE, PRESIDENT OF THE GLOMINOID CORPORATION, MADE HIS WAY DOWNSTAIRS FOR A GLASS OF WARM MILK.

...AND THOSE DAMN REGULATIONS... I THOUGHT THIS WAS A FREE COUNTRY... WE SHOULD SEND ALL THOSE LIBERALS TO RUSSIA!

...WE'VE GOT TO GET SOME SENSIBLE POLITICIANS WHO CAN LISTEN TO REASON, TURN THIS COUNTRY AROUND, GET GOVERNMENT OFF OUR BACKS...

HE TURNED ON THE TELEVISION FOR DISTRACTION.

...WHAT I NEED IS A PROTEGÉ... A MIND I CAN MOLD...

...WE'LL RETURN TO 'DUST ON MY SHOE,' STARRING SPENCER TRACY AND ANNETTE FUNICELLO AFTER THIS MESSAGE...

...THAT'S RIGHT, FOLKS, YOU GET TWELVE GLOW-IN-THE-DARK SOLID PLASTIC COAT HANGERS IN 6 ASSORTED COLORS YOURS FOR ONLY $39.95...

"...JUST SEND YOUR CHECK AND A STAMPED, SELF-ADDRESSED CORRUGATED BOX TO: "HANGLO ENTERPRISES", BOX 999, FLEAFLY, NEBRASKA

"BOX 9...9..." HEY! WHY AM I WRITING THIS? I'VE NO USE FOR SUCH THINGS!...

...IT'S THAT ANNOUNCER... HE'S VERY GIFTED... VERY POISED... CHARISMATIC EVEN...

...Hmmm

ANYBODY WHO CAN SELL GLOW·IN·THE·DARK COAT HANGERS TO ME...

...COULD PROBABLY SELL SUPPLY-SIDE ECONOMICS TO AMERICA!

LATER THAT WEEK HE MET THE ANNOUNCER, A PERSONABLE FELLOW NAMED BOB FOREHEAD.

THESE THINGS YOU'VE TOLD ME ARE VERY DISTURBING, MR. OXBOGGLE. I HAD NO IDEA THERE WAS SO MUCH SUFFERING IN THE "TYCOON SECTOR"

YES, IT'S AWFUL. BUT YOU CAN HELP US.

ME? HOW?

IN CONGRESS.

REALLY?... BUT I HAVE NO POLITICAL EXPERIENCE.

NONSENSE! YOU'RE A NATURAL! AND I'VE GOT YOUR POSITIONS ALL WORKED OUT.

WHAT DOES IT TAKE? LUCK? SKILL? HAPPENSTANCE?

ANDY DUNKENOILER WOULD SURE LIKE TO KNOW.

LOOKS LIKE DUNKENOILER COMING UP THE WALK.

WHAT'S HE RUNNING FOR THIS TIME?

BUT THEY WERE ALWAYS POLITE.

HI, JACK. HI, CAROL. I'M RUNNING FOR CITY COUNCIL AND I'D BE GRATEFUL IF YOU'D SIGN MY PETITION TO GET ON THE BALLOT.

UH, SURE, ANDY.

EVER SINCE ANYONE CAN REMEMBER, ANDY HAS BEEN RUNNING FOR OFFICE. ONE OFFICE OR ANOTHER.

ELECT ANDY DUNKENOILER A MAN FOR THE 50's 60's 70's 80's

HE SEEMS TO BELIEVE HE'S BEEN CALLED. BUT HE NEVER GETS CHOSEN.

COMPARE THAT TO THE CASE OF BOB FOREHEAD:

AS A CHILD, YOUNG BOBBY HAD ONE AMBITION:

TO HOST A T.V. QUIZ SHOW.

...AND NOW IT'S TIME TO PLAY "GROVEL FOR GOODIES" WITH YOUR HOST MONTEE·E·E·E PEARLMOUTH!

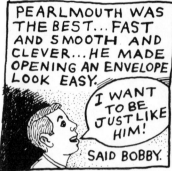
PEARLMOUTH WAS THE BEST... FAST AND SMOOTH AND CLEVER... HE MADE OPENING AN ENVELOPE LOOK EASY.

I WANT TO BE JUST LIKE HIM!

SAID BOBBY.

AND HE PRACTICED EVERY DAY.

LET'S WELCOME OUR NEXT CONTESTANT.

IN COLLEGE HE MAJORED IN POISE, WITH MINORS IN TRIVIA AND PATTER. HE GRADUATED WITH HONORS, BUT QUIZ SHOW JOBS WERE SCARCE. SO HE MODELED MEN'S WEAR AND MADE COMMERCIALS.

THEN ONE DAY:

THE REASON I CALLED YOU, FOREHEAD... I THINK YOU'VE GOT WHAT IT TAKES. YOU COME ACROSS BIG ON T.V. I'VE GOT THE MONEY AND THE PEOPLE TO PUT YOU IN CONGRESS ...AND THAT COULD BE JUST THE BEGINNING.

ANDY DUNKENOILER WOULD HAVE GIVEN HIS MOLARS FOR SUCH AN OPPORTUNITY.

ALL BOB FOREHEAD HAD TO DO WAS SAY "YES."

LET ME THINK ABOUT IT.

HE WENT HOME AND SAT ALONE WITH HIS AUTOGRAPHED PHOTO OF MONTE PEARLMOUTH.

WHAT SHOULD I DO, MONTE? I'M TORN.

HE TALKED IT OVER WITH HIS WIFE.

...THIS COULD MEAN I MIGHT NEVER HOST A QUIZ SHOW.

YES, DEAR, I KNOW. BUT YOU'LL STILL GET TO BE ON T.V. AND QUESTION WITNESSES AT HEARINGS. THE TWO JOBS ARE REALLY VERY SIMILAR. MAYBE IT WAS MEANT TO BE.

MAYBE IT WAS. BECAUSE ONCE HE GOT STARTED, BOB FOREHEAD TOOK TO POLITICS LIKE A MEDFLY TO PINEAPPLE.

ONE DAY GERARD OXBOGGLE INTRODUCED BOB FOREHEAD TO ARTHUR GIGGLE, PROFESSOR OF ECONOMICS AT WHEATTOAST UNIVERSITY IN CALIFORNIA.

BOB HERE IS RUNNING FOR CONGRESS. I'D LIKE YOU TO GIVE HIM SOME ECONOMIC BACKGROUNDING.

MY PLEASURE ...hee-hee.

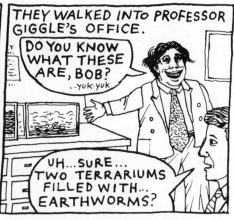

THEY WALKED INTO PROFESSOR GIGGLE'S OFFICE.

DO YOU KNOW WHAT THESE ARE, BOB? ...yuk-yuk

UH...SURE... TWO TERRARIUMS FILLED WITH... EARTHWORMS?

YES, YOU'RE RIGHT. BUT THEY'RE ALSO AN ECONOMETRIC MODEL, WHICH PROVIDES ANSWERS TO THE ECONOMIC ILLS OF OUR SOCIETY. I'LL SHOW YOU WHAT I MEAN. ...giggle...

AT THE BOTTOM OF THE TERRARIUM ON MY LEFT IS A LAYER OF COOKIE CRUMBS...NOW OBSERVE CLOSELY AND TELL ME WHAT YOU SEE. ...heehee...

WELL...THE EARTHWORMS ON THE BOTTOM ARE EATING THE CRUMBS. ...THE REST OF THE WORMS LOOK SKINNY AND UNDERNOURISHED.

THAT'S RIGHT! YOU'RE VERY PERCEPTIVE! ...yukyuk

NOW, IN THIS SECOND TERRARIUM, AS I POUR THE SAME AMOUNT OF CRUMBS OVER THE TOP OF THE WORMS, WHAT DO YOU NOTICE HAPPENING?... BE PATIENT AND WATCH CLOSELY. ...yuk yuk...

WELL...THE WORMS ON THE TOP ARE EATING THE CRUMBS ...AND, AS THEY WIGGLE AROUND, THE UNEATEN CRUMBS ARE TRICKLING DOWN TO THE OTHER WORMS BELOW.

EXACTLY! ...(giggle)

NOW, THAT, YOU SEE, IS EXACTLY HOW OUR ECONOMY WORKS. IF MONEY IS GIVEN TO PEOPLE AT THE BOTTOM, THE REST OF SOCIETY SUFFERS. WHEREAS, IF HUGE TAX BREAKS ARE GIVEN TO LARGE CORPORATIONS, THEN **EVERYBODY** GETS A SHARE! ...hee-hee...

GEE. THAT SOUNDS FAIR.

THIS WAS BOB FOREHEAD'S FIRST EXPOSURE TO THE "GIGGLE WIGGLE," A CONTROVERSIAL THEORY OF ECONOMICS, DISPUTED BY LIBERAL ECONOMISTS AS "UNSCIENTIFIC." FIFTEEN YEARS OF EXPERIMENTS WITH EARTHWORMS AND COOKIE CRUMBS HAD CONVINCED ARTHUR GIGGLE THAT HE WAS RIGHT.

TO EMPHASIZE HIS POINT, PROFESSOR GIGGLE TOOK THE CANDIDATE OUTSIDE TO A BALCONY OVERLOOKING THE OCEAN.

NOW LOOK OUT THERE, BOB...IMAGINE THAT THE OCEAN IS THE CORPORATE SECTOR AND WATCH WHAT HAPPENS TO THE BOATS WHEN THE TIDE COMES IN. ...hee hee...

IT'S...IT'S LIFTING THE BOATS.

THAT'S RIGHT. BUT NOT JUST THE BIG BOATS. **ALL** OF THE BOATS!

GEE WHIZ! YOU'RE RIGHT!

NOW DO YOU UNDERSTAND WHAT'S NEEDED IN OUR ECONOMY?

I...I THINK SO...SURE. IS IT THAT EASY?

YOU BET! ...yuk yuk...

...GOSH. I ALWAYS THOUGHT ECONOMICS WAS COMPLICATED.

NOT AT ALL, BOB. IT'S SIMPLE. **VERY** SIMPLE.

HAW HAW HAW

IT WAS SUBTLE BUT CRITICAL, THE DIFFERENCE IN DEMEANOR BETWEEN A QUIZ SHOW HOST AND A POLITICIAN, AND BOB FOREHEAD WORKED HARD TO CROSS THE GAP.

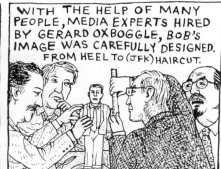

WITH THE HELP OF MANY PEOPLE, MEDIA EXPERTS HIRED BY GERARD OXBOGGLE, BOB'S IMAGE WAS CAREFULLY DESIGNED. FROM HEEL TO (JFK) HAIRCUT.

THEN, IN SPECIAL CRAM SESSIONS, HE MEMORIZED HIS NEW IDENTITY.

WE'VE DECIDED TO MAKE YOU A VORACIOUS READER WITH A SPECIAL PASSION FOR HISTORY AND ECONOMICS,... AS WELL AS DASHIELL HAMMET NOVELS TO SHOW THAT YOU'RE A REGULAR GUY.

WHAT ABOUT MY COMIC BOOKS?

NO! THEY'VE GOT TO GO!

CAN'T I READ THEM ON WEEKENDS, OR PUT THEM IN ESCROW?

ABSOLUTELY NOT.

THIS MAN ➡ IS LEONARD BULLION. WHAT HE SAYS BOB DOES.

LEONARD BULLION IS BOB'S CHARISMATICIAN. A MASTER OF THE SCIENCE OF CHARISMATICS, HE IS CHARGED HERE WITH THE DUTY OF RAISING BOB'S CHARISMA LEVEL.

TODAY WE WORK ON YOUR EYES. THERE ARE 40,000 VOTES IN YOUR EYES ALONE IF YOU LEARN TO USE THEM RIGHT.

ANOTHER ADVISER IS TOM MIMMELMAN, FOREMOST AUTHORITY ON SHIRTSLEEVES.

FOR THE T.V. SPOT, I RECOMMEND A SLEEVE ROLL-UP OF 2 B.E. THAT'S 2 INCHES BELOW THE ELBOW. MY SURVEYS INDICATE THAT MEN WITH SLEEVES AT THIS LEVEL ARE PERCEIVED AS SERIOUS AND HARD WORKING WHILE RETAINING A SENSE OF STYLE THAT IS LOST ABOVE THE ELBOW.

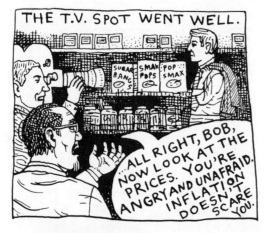

WAS IT "SENSE"

OR HIGH MEGAWATT CHARISMA?

WHICHEVER, IT GOT BOB FOREHEAD A SEAT

IN CONGRESS.

IF YOU WERE A BOOK PUBLISHER TRYING TO TAP THE NERVE CENTER OF THE AMERICAN MARKETPLACE, YOU WOULD PROBABLY BE PUBLISHING: THE OFFICIAL PREPPY CAT BOOK

TO BE FOLLOWED BY: THE OFFICIAL I HATE PREPPY CATS BOOK, THE OFFICIAL BEVERLY HILLS PREPPY CAT DIET BOOK AND 101 USES FOR A DEAD OFFICIAL BEVERLY HILLS PREPPY DIET CAT

IF YOU WERE A POLITICAL STRATEGIST TRYING TO TAP A NERVE CENTER IN THE AMERICAN ELECTORATE, YOU WOULD PROBABLY TRY TO COME UP WITH SOMETHING LIKE: THE BEER AND TELEVISION TAX RELIEF BILL... THAT'S WHAT BOB FOREHEAD'S CONGRESSIONAL STAFF CAME UP WITH...

...AND IT PAID OFF. ...THIS BILL, WHICH I AM INTRODUCING, WOULD ALLOW CONSUMERS TO DEDUCT FROM THEIR INCOME TAX THEIR TOTAL ANNUAL EXPENDITURE FOR BEER AND TELEVISION...

DUMBEST THING I EVER HEARD. SAID ONE HOUSE VETERAN. IT'LL NEVER GET OUT OF COMMITTEE. SAID ANOTHER.

BUT THAT'S NOT WHAT the BEER DRINKERS AND TELEVISION WATCHERS OF AMERICA SAID WHEN TARGETED MAILINGS INFORMED THEM OF the PROPOSED LEGISLATION.

BEVERLY, YOU SHOULD READ THIS!

IN HOMES, AT WORK, AT SOCIAL GATHERINGS, THEY BEGAN TO DISCUSS THE BILL...ITS PLUSES, ITS APPARENT LACK OF MINUSES, AND WHAT IT COULD MEAN FOR THEIR LIVES IF IT PASSED.

I'D BE ABLE TO BUY A NEW SOFA.

I COULD BUY A CAR.

I COULD BUY A HOUSE AND EASILY AFFORD THE INTEREST RATES!

SOON THEY BEGAN TO ORGANIZE...LOCALLY AND THEN NATIONALLY, CALLING THEMSELVES:

THE BEER DRINKERS POLITICAL ACTION COMMITTEE

OR: "SIX PAC."

COORDINATING STRATEGIES WITH THE UNITED TELEVISION WATCHERS, THEY DEMONSTRATED, LOBBIED CONGRESS, AND CONTRIBUTED TO POLITICIANS WHO SUPPORTED THEIR CAUSE.

THE NEWSMEDIA BEGAN COVERING THEM. IT ALSO COVERED BOB FOREHEAD,

AND MADE HIM A NATIONAL FIGURE.

CONGRESSMAN FOREHEAD

CONGRESSMAN!...

REPRESENTATIVE PHILIP CROW.

REPRESENTATIVE DANIEL DUCK.

REPRESENTATIVE JOHN F. KORNBREAD.

...JUST TO NAME A FEW

OF A GROWING NUMBER OF CONGRESSMEN KNOWN AS: "**KENNEDYS OF THE RIGHT.**"

ALL YOUNG, ATTRACTIVE, CONSERVATIVE, AND HIGHLY CHARISMATIC. AT LAST COUNT, NUMBERING NINETEEN.

BRING THEM TOGETHER IN ONE ROOM AND THE EFFECT IS STARTLING.

THAT'S WHAT BOB FOREHEAD DID...

WE'VE GOT SOMETHING POWERFUL HERE, AND WE OUGHT TO MAKE USE OF IT...

HIS STAFF HAD MAPPED OUT THE STRATEGY.

IF WE CAN PUT THIS TOGETHER WITH BOB AT THE HELM, WE COULD WIELD DECISIVE LEVERAGE IN CLOSE FLOOR VOTES.

A FEW MONTHS EARLIER BOB WAS JUST ANOTHER JFK-LOOK-ALIKE ADRIFT IN LEGISLATIVE OBSCURITY. BUT PUBLIC RESPONSE TO HIS "BEER AND TELEVISION TAX RELIEF BILL" (H.R. 895364971526) HAD LIFTED HIM ABOVE THE REST.

...I KNOW YOU ALL WANT TO BE PRESIDENT. SO DO I. BUT RATHER THAN COMPETE WITH EACH OTHER, WHY NOT WORK TOGETHER FOR OUR MUTUAL BENEFIT? MY CHARISMATICIAN TELLS ME THERE IS ENOUGH CHARISMA IN THIS ROOM RIGHT NOW TO PROPEL A LEAR JET FROM LOS ANGELES TO BUFFALO.

...WORKING TOGETHER, WE COULD HELP EACH OTHER AND BECOME PRESIDENT ONE AT A TIME, MAKING EACH OTHER OUR VICE-PRESIDENTS AND APPOINTING OTHERS OF US TO OUR CABINETS AND DOMINATE THE EXECUTIVE BRANCH INTO THE NEXT CENTURY AND PASS THE TORCH TO OUR CHILDREN AND THEIR CHILDREN AND KEEP THE WORLD SAFE FOR SUPPLY SIDE FOR CENTURIES TO COME.

IT'S A BIG JOB. IT WON'T BE EASY...

BUT LET US BEGIN.

THE RESPONSE WAS OVERWHELMING IN THE AFFIRMATIVE.

AND THUS WAS FOUNDED:

THE JFK-LOOK-ALIKE CONSERVATIVE CAUCUS

WITH BOB FOREHEAD AS ITS LEADER.

QUIZ: WHAT IS IT THAT, FOR 50 YEARS LOOKED LIKE THIS:

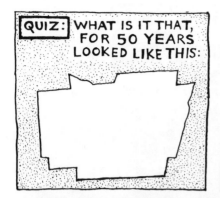

AND NEXT YEAR WILL LOOK LIKE THIS?:

WHAAT?!!

ANSWER: CONGRESSMAN ED BANGER'S CONGRESSIONAL DISTRICT

ARE YOU **SURE** THAT'S MY DISTRICT?!

YOU LIVE RIGHT HERE.

ED IS A DEMOCRAT, A 16-YEAR VETERAN, NEXT IN LINE FOR A FULL COMMITTEE CHAIRMANSHIP.

HOW BAD IS IT?

60% REPUBLICAN.

*

* (EMITTED HERE WAS A DISTURBING GROAN BEYOND THE GRASP OF ONOMATOPOEIA.)

THE RECENT CENSUS REQUIRED THE LEGISLATURE OF ED'S HOME STATE TO REDRAW DISTRICT LINES, ENTITLING ITS REPUBLICAN MAJORITY TO A PLAYFUL SESSION OF FREEHAND DRAWING.

LOOK AT MINE! I'VE GOT **THREE** VETERAN DEMOCRATS IN THE SAME DISTRICT!

THAT'S NOTHING! I'VE GOT THE MAJORITY WHIP IN A DISTRICT THAT'S 80% REPUBLICAN!

PHOOIE! I'VE GOT ONE TO TOP THAT!

WHERE TO SNEEZE: 25 BEST PLACES
TEN LAWYERS TALK ABOUT PAJAMAS
WISHINGTOOWNIAN
SPECIAL: ☆ ☆ ☆
THE STARS OF
Washington
WHERE THEY LIVE
WHAT THEY EAT
HOW THEY WALK
WHAT THEY BREATHE
WHY THEY WERE BORN
AND MORE!

SOUNDS EXCITING, HUH?

WOW! I CAN'T BELIEVE IT! THE SECRETARY OF STATE USES "HALF-AND-HALF" IN HIS COFFEE!

GOSH! IS THAT TRUE?!

LOOK AT THIS! THE DEPUTY ATTORNEY GENERAL OWNS A CAT!

GOLLY! WOW!

IF YOU THINK IT'S EXCITING TO READ, JUST IMAGINE WHAT IT WAS LIKE FOR THE SUBJECTS OF THAT ARTICLE. PEOPLE LIKE THIS MAN, → THE DIRECTOR OF THE OFFICE OF MANGLEMENT OF THE BUDGET.

WOW! IS THAT REALLY HIM?!!

IT SURE IS! HE'S EVEN CARRYING HIS CALCULATOR!

..MAY I HAVE YOUR AUTOGRAPH?

HE'S SO GLAMOROUS! I CAN'T BELIEVE IT!..

HE WAS IN A HURRY TO GET TO HIS OFFICE THAT DAY.

NOW APPEARING
BEFORE THE SENATE BUDGET COMMITTEE ON TUES. & WED.

HIS NEW COMPUTER HAD JUST ARRIVED. HE WAS ANXIOUS TO TRY IT OUT.

BUDGET MASHER

BUDGET MASHER

WHAT DO YOU **MEAN** WE CAN'T DUMP CHEMICALS IN THE RIVER?!!

SAID GERARD OXBOGGLE, PRESIDENT OF THE GLOMINOID CORPORATION.

IT'S AGAINST FEDERAL REGULATIONS.

MAYBE IN **RUSSIA** IT IS, BUT AMERICA **IS A FREE COUNTRY!**

I'M SORRY, SIR, BUT...

IT WAS THEN THAT HE HAD THE ATTACK.

IT'S MINE! IT'S MINE!

IT RAN ITS USUAL COURSE, SENDING HIM RUNNING THROUGH THE STREETS, REACHING and GRABBING IN EVERY DIRECTION.

IT'S MINE! IT'S MINE! EVERYTHING IS MINE!

LATER, IN THE HOSPITAL WHEN THE ATTACK SUBSIDED, MR. OXBOGGLE MADE **ONE** REQUEST.

WHERE'S BOB FOREHEAD?

MEANWHILE, IN WASHINGTON, CONGRESSMAN FOREHEAD WAS FACED WITH A CRISIS OF HIS OWN.

DAN DUCK IS TRYING TO UNDERMINE YOUR LEADERSHIP OF THE LOOK-ALIKE CAUCUS. WE'VE GOT TO FIGHT HIM.

THE CHALLENGE CAUGHT BOB IN A DOUBTFUL MOMENT.

Maybe this isn't my field.

Maybe I should be in L.A., hosting a quiz show.

JUST THEN AN AIDE CAME RUSHING IN.

MR. OXBOGGLE IS IN THE HOSPITAL! HE'S BEEN ASKING FOR YOU!

WHAT?

BOB CAUGHT THE NEXT PLANE. OUTSIDE OXBOGGLE'S ROOM, DOCTORS BRIEFED BOB ON HIS CONDITION.

He suffers from a disease called "MEGALOGLUTTIASIS." ...IN OUR BRAINS, CERTAIN CHEMICAL REACTIONS TELL US WHEN WE HAVE ENOUGH OF SOMETHING. MR. OXBOGGLE IS DEFICIENT IN THESE CHEMICALS. THUS, HE CAN NEVER FEEL SATISFIED WITH HIS MATERIAL STATUS.

THERE IS NO KNOWN CURE, BUT A PROGRAM OF STEADY EXPANSION AND ACQUISITION IS THE BEST TREATMENT WE'VE FOUND.

IF BOB HAD ANY DOUBTS ABOUT THE OPPRESSION OF BIG GOVERNMENT, HIS VISIT WITH ONE OF ITS VICTIMS QUICKLY DISPELLED THEM.

IT'S THOSE... (GROAN) R-REGULATIONS...

THERE-THERE... NOW YOU JUST REST.

LEAVING THE HOSPITAL, BOB FELT INSIDE HIM A NEW RESOLVE FOR THE JOB AHEAD.

BOB FOREHEAD'S VISIT WITH GERARD OX-BOGGLE IN THE HOSPITAL HAD A PROFOUND EFFECT ON THE YOUNG CONGRESSMAN.

I'M BEGINNING TO SEE WHAT'S GOING ON...

IT'S UNCONSCIONABLE WHAT BIG GOVERNMENT IS DOING... ALL THESE GIVEAWAYS TO POOR PEOPLE AND THE UNEMPLOYED WHILE TYING THE HANDS OF BIG CORPORATIONS.

HOW CAN WE EVER EXPECT ANYTHING TO TRICKLE DOWN IF WE'RE CONSTANTLY PUNISHING THE TYCOON SECTOR? I'M BEGINNING TO UNDERSTAND THE REAL MEANING OF THE "GIGGLE WIGGLE."

LOOKING AT MR. OXBOGGLE THERE IN THAT HOSPITAL, MY MIND KEPT GOING BACK TO THE SKINNY, UNDERNOURISHED EARTHWORMS IN THE FIRST TERRARIUM OF PROFESSOR GIGGLE'S ECONOMETRIC MODEL... THE SUPPLY SIDE IS STARVING. I SEE THAT NOW. IT HAS A BIG APPETITE.

THOSE OVERZEALOUS REGULATORS ARE INHIBITING MR. OXBOGGLE.

HE'S A SENSITIVE MAN. ALL HE WANTS IS TO DUMP SOME CHEMICALS IN A RIVER. HE'S NOT ASKING TO OWN OR CONTROL THE WHOLE RIVER. HE'S WILLING TO SHARE IT. IF PEOPLE WANT TO SWIM OR FISH OR GO BOATING IN THAT SAME RIVER, HE'S WILLING TO LET THEM.

ONE DAY BOB FOREHEAD MADE A SPEECH AGAINST BIG GOVERNMENT.

LATER THAT WEEK HE RECEIVED A CALL FROM SENATOR CLANCY FUMES.

WE SHOULD TALK.

Congressional Record

THEY MET FOR LUNCH.

I SEE YOU'VE ACQUIRED SOME INFLUENCE IN THE HOUSE WITH YOUR LOOK-ALIKE CAUCUS. I MIGHT BE ABLE TO HELP YOU ON THE SENATE SIDE.

AND VICE VERSA, OF COURSE.

COMING FROM TOBACCO COUNTRY, AS I DO, I'VE SEEN FIRST HAND THE ABUSE OF GOVERNMENT POWER IN ITS SLANDER OF THE CIGARETTE INDUSTRY. BUT I KNOW WHO'S BEHIND IT...

THE SAME SECULAR HUMANIST LIBERALS WHO FORCE SEX EDUCATION ON OUR CHILDREN.

I'VE INTRODUCED A BILL IN THE SENATE THAT WOULD ELIMINATE SEX EDUCATION FROM PUBLIC SCHOOLS AND REPLACE IT WITH SMOKER EDUCATION.

AFTER THEIR LUNCH, SENATOR FUMES DROVE BOB FOREHEAD ACROSS TOWN.

THERE'S SOMEONE I WANT YOU TO MEET.

TAXI

BATHTUB CAB CO.

FOR MANY YEARS, I WAS DISTURBED BY THE OMISSION FROM OUR CONSTITUTION OF STRONG POSITIONS ON THE CRITICAL SOCIAL ISSUES, LIKE CREATIONISM, TOBACCO ALLOTMENTS, AND THE QUESTION OF WHEN LIFE BEGINS.

AND, OF COURSE, THE COURTS WERE GIVEN TOO MUCH POWER... IT LEFT US VULNERABLE TO A SECULAR HUMANIST TAKEOVER. ... I USED TO READ AND REREAD THE CONSTITUTION. I JUST KNEW THERE WAS MORE THERE THAN MEETS THE EYE.

THEN ONE DAY I MET A MAN WHO VERIFIED MY HUNCH. LET ME INTRODUCE YOU...

HI, SAM. THIS IS CONGRESSMAN FOREHEAD. I'D LIKE YOU TO SHOW HIM YOUR FINDINGS.

THE SUPREME COURT IS COMMUNIST PLOT BY RUSSIAN AGENTS BEGINNING IN STIT

RUSSIAN SPIES TRIED TO WRITE OUR CONSTITUTION. CRYPTOGRAPHY REVEALS ITS TRUE MEANING.

DON CON OF AGE GOV SPI

BEWARE LIES AN INACCU MISINTE RUSSIAN TO CON

THE CONSTITUTIONAL CONVENTION OF 1787 WAS INFILTRATED BY RUSSIAN SPIES. THE MOST IMPORTANT PROVISIONS HAD TO BE WRITTEN IN CODE.

I RECENTLY DECIPHERED A SECTION THAT GIVES CONGRESS THE POWER TO DISBAND THE SUPREME COURT "IF IT FEELS LIKE IT."

I FEEL LIKE IT. HOW ABOUT YOU, BOB?

WE COULD REPLACE THEM WITH A PANEL OF EVANGELISTS. ... SAY, THE 3 OR 4 WITH THE HIGHEST NIELSEN RATINGS.

Well... I'VE GOT TO GET BACK TO MY OFFICE NOW... BUT I'LL GIVE IT SOME THOUGHT.

LATER: SENATOR FUMES HAS BIG PLANS.

YES. AND A BIG MAILING LIST.

ONE EVENING CONGRESS MET IN JOINT SESSION TO HEAR THE PRESIDENT SPEAK.

THEY REMEMBERED THE AMBITIOUS GOALS OF HIS CAMPAIGN...

...I PROMISE to ELIMINATE THE FEDERAL GOVERNMENT BY 1984...

BUT ONCE IN OFFICE, HIS GOALS HAD ALTERED A BIT. SOME SENATORS AND CONGRESSMEN HAD BEEN SHOWN DIAGRAMS OF HIS VARIOUS PROPOSALS FOR REORGANIZING THE GOVERNMENT:

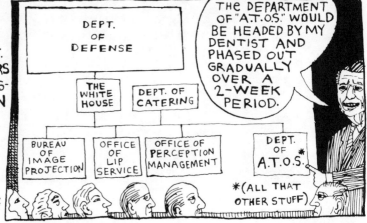

DEPT. OF DEFENSE

THE WHITE HOUSE

DEPT. OF CATERING

BUREAU OF IMAGE PROJECTION

OFFICE OF LIP SERVICE

OFFICE OF PERCEPTION MANAGEMENT

DEPT. OF A.T.O.S.

THE DEPARTMENT OF "A.T.O.S." WOULD BE HEADED BY MY DENTIST AND PHASED OUT GRADUALLY OVER A 2-WEEK PERIOD.

*(ALL THAT OTHER STUFF)

RECENTLY A NEW PROPOSAL WAS IN THE WORKS. THIS SPEECH WOULD UNVEIL IT.

WHAT I AM PROPOSING IS THAT WE, AT THE FEDERAL LEVEL, DEFER ALL RESPONSIBILITY FOR SOCIAL PROBLEMS FOR A PERIOD OF 8 YEARS.

...DURING THIS TIME, THE STATES MAY, IF THEY CHOOSE, TAKE ON THE BURDEN, OR DEFER IT ALSO.

IF THE STATES FOLLOW OUR EXAMPLE, THEN THOSE POOR AND UNDERPRIVILEGED PEOPLE WHO FIND THEIR CONDITIONS INTOLERABLE WILL HAVE THE OPPORTUNITY TO VOTE WITH THEIR FEET AND MOVE TO CANADA.

BY THE END OF THE 8-YEAR PERIOD, SURELY MOST, IF NOT ALL, OF THEM WILL BE GONE,...

...AND WE WILL HAVE ELIMINATED **BOTH** POVERTY AND BIG GOVERNMENT IN A SINGLE, BOLD STROKE.

..WE CALL THIS POLICY **"THE NEW DEFERRALISM".** I HOPE YOU WILL SUPPORT IT.

THERE WAS TREMENDOUS APPLAUSE.

The PRESIDENT SHOOK MANY HANDS AS HE MADE HIS WAY OUT OF THE CHAMBER. BOB FOREHEAD WATCHED HIM.

HE WAS HAPPY FOR THE PRESIDENT. ANOTHER THING HE FELT WAS...

JEALOUSY.

CROWDED AROUND A DOOR in the WHITE HOUSE PRESS ROOM, REPORTERS, PHOTOGRAPHERS, and T.V. camera CREWS AWAITED ADMITTANCE TO A "PHOTO OPPORTUNITY."

ARE THEY REALLY INLAID WITH DIAMONDS?

DIAMONDS AND GOLD, I HEAR.

WORTH $2,000.00 A PIECE!

FINALLY the DOOR WAS OPENED. THEY HURRIED DOWN the WALKWAY to the EAST WING...

...and GOT their FIRST view OF the NEW WHITE HOUSE SALT and PEPPER SHAKERS.

AMONG the REPORTERS was MALCOLM FRAZZLE, WASHINGTON CORRESPONDENT FOR "DISHWASHER MONTHLY," a popular tRADE JOURNAL.

HE WAS MAKING NOTES FOR A PUFF PIECE WHEN SUDDENLY:

PSSSSSST!

DON'T LOOK AT ME. I HAVE INFORMATION FOR YOU. MEET ME AT 6:00 at the FUDGEKISS monument.

They met AS PLANNED.

I am the DEPUTY ASSISTANT to the DIRECTOR OF DISH MAINTENANCE!

I STUDIED DISHWASHING AT the SLUSHBONNE ACADEMY IN PARIS. I HAVE MY DOCTORATE.

GENERAL FUDGEKISS

THE NEW DISHES PURCHASED BY THIS ADMINISTRATION REQUIRE SPECIAL CARE. THIS WILL LEAD TO EXORBITANT COST OVERRUNS AND EXACERBATE THE DEFICIT.

GENERA FUDGEK

SOUNDS SERIOUS.

OBSERVED MALCOLM, PULLING OUT HIS NOTE PAD.

MEANWHILE, IN BOB FOREHEAD'S OFFICE:

THAT SALT AND PEPPER SET IS GETTING MORE PRESS COVERAGE THAN I AM THESE DAYS.

©1982 m.a.s.

MALCOLM FRAZZLE, WASHINGTON CORRESPONDENT FOR "DISHWASHER MONTHLY," MET SECRETLY WITH THE WHITE HOUSE KITCHEN STAFFER ON SEVERAL OCCASIONS.

THE NEW WHITE HOUSE DISHES REQUIRE SPECIAL CARE!

GENERAL FUDGEKISS

ORDINARY DETERGENTS CANNOT BE USED. THEY WOULD HARM THE PRECIOUS METALS AND JEWELS INLAID INTO THE DISHES. SO A SPECIALLY-BLENDED CLEANSER MUST BE IMPORTED FROM THE FAR EAST.

and then, OF COURSE, THERE'S THE DISHWASHER.

GENERAL FUDGEKISS

RECENTLY, A CONTRACT WAS SECRETLY AWARDED TO THE GLOMINOID CORPORATION TO DESIGN AND BUILD AN AUTOMATIC DISHWASHER CAPABLE OF WASHING THE NEW DISHES SAFELY. THE COST WILL BE ENORMOUS, EXCEEDING THE BUDGET CEILING.

THERE IS STRONG DISAGREEMENT AMONG THE KITCHEN STAFF OVER THIS AND OTHER POLICY DECISIONS.

I OPPOSE THE PURCHASE OF THIS DISHWASHER. THE AMERICAN PEOPLE SHOULD BE TOLD ABOUT IT WHILE THEY STILL CAN BE.

BY NEXT SUMMER THE ADMINISTRATION WILL INTRODUCE "THE FREEDOM OF CLASSIFICATION ACT," WHICH WOULD ALLOW THEM TO CLASSIFY AS "TOP SECRET" ANY INFORMATION THAT ENDANGERS PRESIDENTIAL PRESTIGE. THIS WOULD FALL UNDER THAT CATEGORY.

MALCOLM HURRIED BACK TO HIS OFFICE.

HE WASN'T SURE WHICH TO WRITE FIRST: THE ARTICLE OR HIS PULITZER PRIZE ACCEPTANCE SPEECH.

I GUESS I OUGHT TO WRITE THE ARTICLE FIRST.

THE FIRST COPIES ARRIVED BY MAIL. TO SUBSCRIBERS.

A QUARTER OF A MILLION DOLLARS FOR A DISHWASHER?!!

AND THAT'S ONLY AN ESTIMATE.

DISHWASHER MONTHLY

THEN THE WIRE SERVICES PICKED IT UP. AND T.V. AND RADIO.

WYAP-TV CRASHBANG NEWS

ACCORDING TO A STORY IN "DISHWASHER MONTHLY, THE WHITE HOUSE WILL EXACERBATE the DEFICIT WITH the PURCHASE OF THE MOST EXPENSIVE DISHWASHER IN HISTORY.

WYAP-

©1982 MAS

THE STORY CAME AT A BAD TIME FOR the WHITE HOUSE STAFF.

THE CHIEF ADVISERS WERE EXHAUSTED FROM A LONG DAY OF TRYING TO GET the PRESIDENT INTERESTED IN FOREIGN POLICY.

He seems to Listen to the PARTS ABOUT the SOVIET THREAT.

I THINK SO. HE'S JUST NOT INTERESTED IN DETAILS ...LIKE EUROPE.

...AND CHINA.

AND THE MIDDLE EAST. ...AND

THE DISHWASHER STORY THREW THE WHITE HOUSE INTO A PANIC. THEY STONEWALLED THE PRESS.

COME ON. OPEN UP!

HM-MM.

BEHIND THE SCENES, THEY SEARCHED FOR THE SOURCE OF the LEAK.

MEANWHILE, ON CAPITOL HILL, CRITICS OF THE PRESIDENT'S BUDGET LAUNCHED THEIR STRONGEST ATTACKS, HAMMERING AWAY AT THE DEFICIT.

IN VIEW OF ITS POLICY OF SEVERE CUTBACKS, IT IS A DISGRACE TO SEE THIS ADMINISTRATION WASHING ITS DISHES ON THE BACKS OF THE POOR.

CONGRESSMAN BOB FOREHEAD WAS A SUPPORTER OF THE PRESIDENT.

BUT, MORE THAN THAT, HE WAS A SUPPORTER OF BOB FOREHEAD.

AND A DISCIPLE OF ARTHUR GIGGLE, WHO PROMPTED HIM TO ADDRESS THE HOUSE.

THE ONLY WAY TO GET RID OF OUR DEFICIT IS TO CUT MORE TAXES. ONLY WHEN GOVERNMENT HAS NO MONEY TO SPEND WILL IT STOP SPENDING.

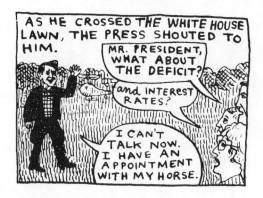

THE PRESIDENT NEVER HAD ANY TROUBLE GETTING ON TELEVISION.

BUT LATELY BOB FOREHEAD DID.

I HAVEN'T HAD ANY PRESS COVERAGE FOR FIVE WEEKS. I'M BEGINNING TO FEEL INVISIBLE.

IF I WERE PRESIDENT, I WOULD GET PLENTY OF PRESS COVERAGE.

THIS WAS THE FIRST TIME HE'D EVER SAID THIS. IT WOULDN'T BE THE LAST TIME.

IT WASN'T WORKING THE WAY IT USED TO.

I NEED YOUR HELP ON THIS ONE, JOHN.

"JOHN" IS CONGRESSMAN JOHN GASVALVE, AN INFLUENTIAL HOUSE REPUBLICAN.

LAST SUMMER HE'D SAT IN THAT SAME CHAIR, MELTED INTO PUTTY BY THE "POWERS OF PERSUASION" OF THE "GREAT COMMUNICATOR."

BUT NOW, DESPITE THE HEADY ATMOSPHERE OF THE OVAL OFFICE AND THE UNRELENTING PERSONAL WARMTH OF ITS OCCUPANT, THINGS HAD CHANGED.

I'M SORRY, MR. PRESIDENT, BUT I THINK YOU'LL HAVE TO BEND ON THE BUDGET.

THE PRESIDENT DIDN'T TAKE WELL TO THIS.

"BEND"?...

DICTIONARY

LATER THAT WEEK AT A PRESS CONFERENCE, HE GOT A CHANCE TO DEFEND HIS BUDGET.

MR. PRESIDENT, MANY ECONOMISTS BELIEVE YOUR HUGE DEFICITS WILL PERPETUATE HIGH INTEREST RATES. HOW DO YOU RESPOND?

I'VE HEARD A LOT OF WHINING ABOUT HIGH INTEREST RATES FROM the SOB SISTERS IN the HOUSING AND AUTO INDUSTRIES and I'D LIKE to POINT OUT SOMETHING ON the POSITIVE SIDE.

WITH THAT, HE PULLED OUT AN INDEX CARD.

WE JUST RECENTLY RECEIVED WORD OF A MAN WHO GOT A LOAN TO BUY A NEW AUTOMOBILE MANY YEARS AGO WHEN INTEREST RATES WERE LOW.

WELL, THAT MAN USED THAT AUTOMOBILE AS A GETAWAY CAR IN SEVERAL ARMED ROBBERIES.

BUT I'M HAPPY TO SAY THAT OUR CURRENT HIGH INTEREST RATES MAKE AUTOMOBILES UNAFFORDABLE TO A MAN IN HIS INCOME BRACKET!

THE REPORTERS DID NOT SEEM IMPRESSED. IF ANYTHING, THEY LOOKED CONFUSED. BUT THEY DUTIFULLY MADE NOTES OF THE REMARK.

ANOTHER PERSON MAKING NOTES WAS A POLITICAL STRATEGIST FOR BOB FOREHEAD.

HE'S BEGINNING TO LOSE MOMENTUM. WE MAY HAVE A SHOT AT '84.

WINDING *and* STRETCHING FOR OVER A MILE ALONG the POTOMAC RIVER IS the FABULOUS **LAYERCAKE** HOTEL/APARTMENT/BOUTIQUE COMPLEX, HOME OF the RICH, the POWERFUL, the FAMOUS.

ONE EVENING *at* the **LAYERCAKE** THE MR. *and* MRS. **RICHARD HOINBOINS** HOSTED *an* ELABORATELY CATERED RECEPTION FOR their DEAR FRIENDS *and* NEIGHBORS the MR. *and* MRS. **REGINALD R. DOORWINGS** ON the OCCASION OF their POODLE'S THIRD HAIRCUT.

CONGRATULATIONS, REG! THE THIRD ONE IS A BIG ONE.

THANKS, JIM. WE'RE JUST VERY HAPPY.

THE LIST OF GUESTS WAS ENORMOUS ...AMBASSADORS, SENATORS, GENERALS, TITANS OF INDUSTRY...

...AMONG THEM: GERARD V. OXBOGGLE, PRESIDENT OF the GLOMINOID CORPORATION, ...*and* OTHERS.

THEY GOT INTO A DISCUSSION OF WEAPONRY.

I'm DISTURBED ABOUT THAT BOMB THAT PRESERVES BUILDINGS BUT KILLS PEOPLE INDISCRIMINATELY. IT NEEDS TO BE PERFECTED. AS IS, IT COULD WIPE OUT HUGE SECTORS OF OUR INTERNATIONAL MARKETPLACE.

IT WAS A CASUAL CONVERSATION BUT IT LED TO SERIOUS TALKS BE-TWEEN MR. OXBOGGLE, VARIOUS SCIENTISTS AND THE DEPARTMENT OF DEFENSE...

...RESULTING IN "PROJECT CCB".

...THE TECHNOLOGY EXISTS TO DEVELOP A BOMB THAT WILL KILL ONLY THOSE PEOPLE WHO DO NOT CARRY A CREDIT CARD.

AT A SECRET LOCATION, WORK WAS BEGUN ON THE CREDIT CARD BOMB.

©1982 M.A.S.

ONCE A WEEK GERARD OXBOGGLE, PRESIDENT OF THE GLOMINOID CORPORATION, VISITS THE JUSTICE DEPARTMENT...

THE UNITED STATES DEPARTMENT OF JUSTICE

© 1982 m.a.s

...FOR A SESSION WITH HIS MERGER THERAPIST.

...NOW DESCRIBE TO ME THE FEELINGS...

MERGER THERAPY WAS DEVELOPED BY THE JUSTICE DEPARTMENT IN 1981.

IT'S A KIND OF ANXIETY.

YES, YES.

OR, WORSE THAN THAT, IT'S GUILT.

MM-HM...

IT COMES OVER ME EVERY TIME I TRY TO BUY OUT ANOTHER CORPORATION. I START TO HEAR VOICES IN MY HEAD, TAUNTING ME, THREATENING TO TAKE ME TO COURT.

DO YOU KNOW WHOSE VOICES THEY ARE?

THEY'RE ... THEY'RE OLD VOICES FROM THE PAST, FROM THE OLD ANTITRUST DIVISION...

THAT'S RIGHT! VERY GOOD! NOW REMEMBER: THOSE VOICES AREN'T REAL ANYMORE. THE NEW JUSTICE DEPARTMENT IS YOUR FRIEND. NOW LET'S SEE YOU RE-LEASE THOSE INHI-BITIONS.

YES, BUT...

DON'T GIVE ME "YES, BUT." LET GO! LET GO OF THE PAST! OPEN YOUR HORIZONS!

...ALL THINGS ARE POSSIBLE NOW... I WANT YOU TO DO AN EXERCISE. I WANT YOU TO TELL ME YOUR FANTASY, A MERGER FAN-TASY OF THE MERGER OF YOUR DREAMS.

A FEW MO-MENTS PASS-ED. MR. OXBOG-GLE GOT INTO IT.

WELL, WHAT I'D LIKE TO DO IS TO KEEP MERGING AND MERG-ING AND MERGING UNTIL I OWN CONTROL-LING INTEREST IN EVERY MAJOR COR-PORATION...

...THEN I'D LIKE TO BUY OUT THE FEDERAL GOVERNMENT AND OPERATE IT AS A SUBSIDIARY... AND THEN...

AFTER HIS SESSION, MR. OXBOGGLE FELT CHEERFUL.

NEXT WEEK WE'LL WORK ON MAKING IT HAPPEN.

ONE DAY A PENTAGON OFFICIAL TESTIFIED BEFORE A SENATE COMMITTEE.

WE HAVE DEVELOPED A NEW STRATEGIC WEAPONS POLICY FOR THE COMING DECADES.

WE CALL THIS APPROACH THE "MOR-XS", A TWO-PRONGED STRATEGY FOR THE ACHIEVEMENT OF "MULTI-ORNAMENTATIONAL REDUNDANCY" THROUGH A PROCESS OF "EXPERIMENTAL SPENDING."

THE PURPOSE OF THE PROGRAM IS DETERRENCE. WE MUST RETAIN THE CAPABILITY TO DETER THE SOVIETS BEFORE THEY DETER US... TO DETER THEM TO KINGDOM COME IF NECESSARY...

AFTER READING HIS PREPARED STATEMENT, THE WITNESS WAS QUESTIONED BY COMMITTEE MEMBERS. AMONG THEM: SENATOR STEVE DENIM.

I RECOGNIZE THE NEED FOR NATIONAL DEFENSE, BUT I'M ALSO CONCERNED ABOUT DEFICIT SPENDING AND THE DAMAGING EFFECT IT HAS ON OUR ECONOMY.

SEN. DENIM

THAT DAMAGING EFFECT IS PART OF OUR STRATEGY, SENATOR. IT DEMONSTRATES OUR RESOLVE.

AT PRESENT, HOWEVER, SOVIET DEFENSE SPENDING CAUSES 85% MORE DAMAGE TO THE SOVIET ECONOMY THAN U.S. DEFENSE SPENDING CAUSES TO THE U.S. ECONOMY. THIS GAP IS UNACCEPTABLE. IT MUST BE CLOSED.

SENATOR DENIM APPEARED SKEPTICAL. HIS QUESTIONS CHALLENGED THE POLICY.

©1982 MAS

AS HE SPOKE, HIS WORDS AND ATTITUDES WERE MADE NOTE OF...

...BY JANE FLETTERMINK.

JANE WORKS FOR THE GLOMINOID CORPORATION, A MAJOR DEFENSE CONTRACTOR. HER JOB IS TO MONITOR SENATE HEARINGS AND REPORT BACK ON THE ATTITUDES OF VARIOUS SENATORS.

LATER THAT DAY:

SENATOR DENIM SEEMS TO BE OPPOSED TO THE NEW WEAPONS SYSTEMS.

HMM... HE'S BEEN GIVING US A LOT OF TROUBLE LATELY...

BUT WE'LL FIX HIM IN THE NEXT ELECTION.

ONE EVENING, AFTER A TEDIOUS DAY ON CAPITOL HILL, CONGRESSMAN BOB FOREHEAD WATCHED A T.V. QUIZ SHOW.

AND, MRS. NOW, MRS. LARBLEMAN, FOR 3,000 DOLLARS...

I'M BETTER THAN THAT GUY!

...NAME THREE BUSDRIVERS FROM AKRON, OHIO"
...TICK...
...TICK...
...TICK...

HE'S GOT NO STYLE... ...I COULD HOST **CIRCLES** AROUND HIM!

"UM...UH... WALTER AUKBUNX ...UM...UM... TOM SWORGLES... ...UM... AND UM..."

BZZZT!

MEANWHILE, HE'S ON T.V. EVERY WEEK AND I'M...

©1982 MAS

...IN THE WRONG BUSINESS!

"I'M SORRY, MRS. LARBLEMAN. IT WAS ROGER GANKBURN. BUT YOU STILL GET TO KEEP YOUR TICKET STUB. THANK..."

IT WAS A SUDDEN IMPULSE. PERHAPS HE'D SAT THROUGH ONE SHRIMPBOAT REGULATIONS HEARING TOO MANY. HE BEGAN PACKING A SUITCASE. HE TOLD ONLY HIS WIFE.

WHAT ARE YOU GOING TO DO IN LOS ANGELES?

FIND A JOB HOSTING A QUIZ SHOW. IT'S IN MY BLOOD. I CAN'T DENY IT.

THIS CONGRESS JOB IS A WASH-OUT I HAVEN'T BEEN ON T.V. IN 2½ MONTHS!

I'M TIRED OF WAITING AROUND TO BE PRESIDENT. IT TAKES TOO LONG. I WANT TO BE ON TELEVISION NOW!

I'LL SEND FOR YOU AND THE KIDS AS SOON AS I GET SETTLED.

THE NEXT DAY, HOWEVER, BOB FOREHEAD'S STAFF HAD NO IDEA OF WHERE HE WAS.

I HAVEN'T SEEN HIM.

NEITHER HAVE I.

UPON HIS ARRIVAL IN LOS ANGELES, BOB FOREHEAD WENT TO SEE AN AGENT WHO USED TO GET HIM WORK IN T.V. COMMERCIALS.

I WANT TO HOST A QUIZ SHOW, MARTY. YOU GOT ANYTHING FOR ME?

MAYBE ONE OR TWO POSSIBILITIES...

...BUT I THOUGHT YOU WERE A CONGRESSMAN.

WELL, TECHNICALLY I STILL AM. ...IT PAYS THE BILLS FOR NOW, BUT I NEED TO MOVE ON.

I HEARD TALK YOU WERE IN LINE TO BE PRESIDENT. NOW THAT'S A GOOD JOB. IT WOULD REALLY GET YOUR NAME AROUND.

I CAN'T WAIT THAT LONG, MARTY...AND THERE WAS NO GUARANTEE...AND YOU DON'T KNOW WHAT IT'S LIKE TO SIT THROUGH THOSE HEARINGS...

MEANWHILE, BACK IN WASHINGTON, BOB'S CONGRESSIONAL STAFF WAS FRANTIC.

HAVE YOU FOUND OUT WHERE HE IS YET?

HIS WIFE SAYS HE'S IN CALIFORNIA.

CALIFORNIA?! ...BUT HE'S SCHEDULED TO ADDRESS THE CONVENTION OF THE NATIONAL ASSOCIATION OF MOLDING CUTTERS DOWNTOWN TONIGHT!

SHE SAID HE'S LOOKING FOR A JOB IN TELEVISION.

THAT EVENING TWO OF BOB'S AIDES CAUGHT A PLANE TO L.A. TO LOOK FOR THEIR BOSS.

MEANWHILE, IN DOWNTOWN WASHINGTON, AT THE NATIONAL ASSOCIATION OF MOLDING CUTTERS CONVENTION:

...AND NOW, LADIES AND GENTLEMEN, CONGRESSMAN BOB FOREHEAD.

CLAPCLAPCLAPCLAPCLAPCLAP CLAP CLAP CLAP CLAP CLAP CLAP

I COME BEFORE YOU TODAY TO PAY TRIBUTE TO THE GREAT AND HISTORIC CONTRIBUTION OF AMERICA'S MOLDING CUTTERS.

THE SPEECH LASTED 23 MINUTES.

...IN THESE TROUBLED TIMES AMERICA LOOKS ONCE AGAIN TO ITS MOLDING CUTTERS TO SET AN EXAMPLE OF COURAGE AND HOPE...

THE SPEECH WENT OVER BIG. ONLY BOB FOREHEAD'S STAFF KNEW THAT THE SPEAKER WAS NOT BOB FOREHEAD, BUT, RATHER, CONGRESSMAN JOHN KORNBREAD, A FELLOW JFK LOOK-ALIKE.

THANK YOU, JOHN.

HE OWES ME A BIG ONE FOR THIS.

JUST BEYOND THE BORDER OF THE DISTRICT OF COLUMBIA, IN BETHESDA MARYLAND, IS LOCATED: THE MARYLAND INSTITUTE OF PERCEPTRONICS.

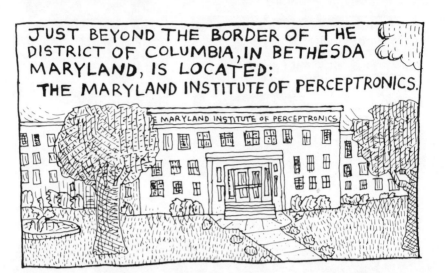

THE MARYLAND INSTITUTE OF PERCEPTRONICS

FOUNDED ON THE PRINCIPLE THAT "PERCEPTION IS REALITY," IN POLITICS AND IN LIFE, THE INSTITUTE IS DEDICATED TO THE SCIENTIFIC MANIPULATION OF PERCEPTIONS.

LONGITUDINAL PERCEPTRONIC DEACTIVIZATION TABLE XII SERIES 5

PLOTTING OF PERCEP...IC WAVELEN...

IF A POLITICIAN DELIVERS A SPEECH IN THE MIDDLE OF A FOREST AND NO ONE HEARS IT,...

ASKS A PROFESSOR OF A FRESHMEN CLASS,

...WILL HE GET ELECTED?

OFFERING COURSES and DEGREES in SUCH AREAS AS CHARISMA theory, APPLIED CHARISMATICS, and PERCEPTUAL ENGINEERING, the INSTITUTE HAS PRODUCED A SIGNIFICANT PERCENTAGE OF BEHIND-the-SCENES MANIPULATORS OF OUR PRESENT DAY SOCIETY.

PERCEPTOGRAPHIC CHARISMETER CHART:

PERCEPTOGRAPH

CHA...TER

AMONG *them*: DR. DWIGHT LIDLUD, A PERCEPTUAL ENGINEER.

PHOOIE!

DWIGHT WORKS FOR CONGRESSMAN BOB FOREHEAD. HE WAS VERY UPSET WHEN BOB RAN OFF TO L.A.

IT'S **MY** FAULT! HE *needed* BETTER BUZZWORDS.

DWIGHT IS A BUZZWORD SPECIALIST.

DON'T BLAME YOURSELF, DWIGHT.

...HE NEEDED **MORE** THAN BUZZWORDS. ..HE NEEDED FUZZWORDS!

©1982 M.A.S.

WHAT ARE "FUZZWORDS"?

ASKED AN AIDE TO CONGRESSMAN BOB FOREHEAD.

DWIGHT LIDLUD, BOB'S CHIEF PERCEPTUAL ENGINEER, TRIED TO EXPLAIN.

OVER THE PAST FEW YEARS I'VE HAD BOB USE A LOT OF BUZZWORDS LIKE "JOBS", "PROSPERITY" and "BIG SPENDERS" ... THEY WORKED FOR A WHILE...

LATELY, *however*, I'VE DETECTED an EMERGING PERCEPTION OF BOB AS BEING PURELY IMAGE AND LACKING IN SUBSTANCE.

WE'VE GOT TO COUNTER THIS "PURELY-IMAGE" IMAGE WITH AN IMAGE OF BOB AS HAVING *an* IN-DEPTH GRASP OF ISSUES.

FUZZWORDS CAN DO THIS.

...THE VAST MAJORITY OF AMERICANS ARE VERY UPSET ABOUT OUR ECONOMY. THEY ARE ALSO VERY FUZZY-MINDED ABOUT WHAT SHOULD BE DONE OR EVEN WHAT EXACTLY IS CAUSING THE PROBLEMS.

TAXI

SOFA CAB CO.

WHENEVER THEY TRY TO FIGURE IT OUT, THEY BECOME ENGULFED IN A VAST MENTAL FUZZINESS.

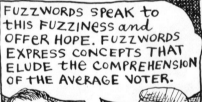

FUZZWORDS SPEAK TO THIS FUZZINESS *and* OFFER HOPE. FUZZWORDS EXPRESS CONCEPTS THAT ELUDE THE COMPREHENSION OF THE AVERAGE VOTER.

BOB, FOR INSTANCE, MIGHT URGE A "NON-INTERVENTIONIST MONETARY POLICY" OR CALL FOR THE FEDERAL RESERVE TO "ABANDON ITS TARGETS OF AGGREGATES".

IF SPOKEN WITH AN AIR OF CONFIDENT AUTHORITY, FUZZWORDS LIKE THESE COULD ATTRACT MILLIONS OF ANXIOUS, FUZZY-MINDED VOTERS WHO HAVE LOST FAITH IN POLITICIANS WHO USE ONLY BUZZWORDS.

THE AIDE WAS IMPRESSED.

IF ONLY WE COULD LOCATE BOB.

MOST PEOPLE THINK it's the SECRETARY OF STATE, the ATTORNEY GENERAL, OR the NATIONAL SECURITY ADVISER.

BUT WASHINGTON INSIDERS WILL TELL YOU THAT THE MOST IMPORTANT POST IN THE ADMINISTRATION IS OCCUPIED BY THIS MAN:

... BAYARD HOTWALL, PERCEIVER GENERAL OF THE UNITED STATES.

HIS IS A BIG JOB, OVERSEEING THE INDUCEMENT, DEVELOPMENT, and ORCHESTRATION OF THOUSANDS OF PERCEPTIONS EVERY YEAR.

PRESENTLY, PERCEIVER GENERAL HOTWALL IS REVISING THE OFFICIAL UNITED STATES PERCEPTION OF THE SOVIET PERCEPTION OF THE UNITED STATES PERCEPTION OF THE SOVIET STRATEGY FOR NUCLEAR ARMS.

DWIGHT LIDLUD WOULD LIKE TO HAVE HOTWALL'S JOB. WHICH IS WHY HE WORKS FOR BOB FOREHEAD.

IF BOB EVER BECOMES PRESIDENT, HE'D SURELY APPOINT ME PERCEIVER GENERAL.

DARLING, YOU NEED SLEEP.

HOW CAN I SLEEP WHILE BOB IS MISSING? MY WHOLE CAREER IS ON THE LINE!

Meanwhile, in L.A., TWO OF BOB'S AIDES VISITED BOB'S SISTER and FOUND HIM THERE.

BOB!

YOU'VE GOT TO COME BACK TO WASHINGTON QUICK!

I'M NOT GOING BACK. ...I CAN'T TAKE IT.

SAID CONGRESSMAN BOB FOREHEAD.

DO YOU KNOW WHAT IT'S LIKE TO SIT THROUGH THREE WEEKS OF SHRIMPBOAT REGULATIONS HEARINGS WITHOUT A SINGLE CAMERA IN THE ROOM?! ...NOT ONE!

TOMORROW I'VE GOT AN AUDITION FOR A JOB HOSTING A QUIZ SHOW. I'M ONE OF EIGHT FINALISTS. I'VE WAITED ALL MY LIFE FOR THIS.

LATER, BOB'S AIDES PLACED A PHONE CALL TO THEIR WASHINGTON OFFICE.

Phone

...SEND MORE PEOPLE. WE MAY HAVE TO TAKE HIM BY FORCE.

IN WASHINGTON, meanwhile, Dwight Lidlud, BOB's chief Perceptual Engineer, WAS STRUGGLING TO CONCOCT THE RIGHT MIX OF FUZZWORDS and BUZZWORDS capable OF LAUNCHING a new PERCEPTION OF BOB.

As he worked, the usual tight knot formed in his stomach as it always did before the launching of a new perception! And the same question haunted him.

WILL IT FLY?

Meanwhile, in L.A., Bob was auditioning.

Hi, Ladies and Gentlemen.. Welcome to...

Loosen up! Loosen up! You move like a politician!

BOB DIDN'T GET THE JOB.

Come on back to Washington.

said an aide.

NO.

SUDDENLY, BOB WAS SURROUNDED BY STAFFERS. THEY GRABBED HIM, PUSHED HIM INTO A RENTED CAR...

LET ME GO!

...and drove to the airport.

LET ME OUT!

On the PLANE to WASHington, BOB WAS STRANGELY Silent.

WHEN HE GOT HOME HE PULLED OUT HIS PHOTO OF MONTE PEARLMOUTH, QUIZ SHOW HOST and BOB'S CHILDHOOD IDOL.

Well, Monte, I tried...

THE NEXT DAY HE MET WITH DWIGHT LIDLUD.

A "NON-INTERVENTIONIST MONETARY POLICY"? WHAT DOES THAT MEAN?

IT MEANS 15 POINTS IN YOUR POPULARITY RATING IF YOU LEARN TO USE IT RIGHT.

The Annual Convention OF THE national ASSOCIATION OF Wall Socket ADJUSTERS PROVIDED AN IDEAL TESTING GROUND FOR BOB'S NEW FUZZWORDS,

... FOR DWIGHT HAD DETECTED among THEM PRECISELY THE PERCEPTION HE WAS TRYING TO COUNTERACT.

IT SAYS HERE CONGRESSMAN FOREHEAD WILL ADDRESS US.

NOT THAT GUY!.. HE'S PURE SHOW BIZ.

THEN CAME THE FUZZWORDS.

... THE FEDERAL RESERVE MUST ABANDON ITS TARGETS OF AGGREGATES, AND ALSO...

WHAT DOES THAT MEAN?

I DON'T KNOW, BUT I THINK HE'S RIGHT.

DWIGHT WATCHED THE AUDIENCE CLOSELY. IT WAS SUBTLE BUT CLEAR... THAT HUNGRY LOOK IN THEIR FACES... THAT DESIRE TO SURRENDER... TO BELIEVE... TO BE LED...

IT'S WORKING.

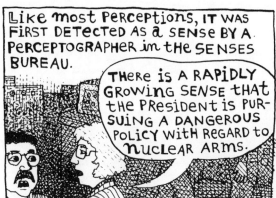

Like most perceptions, it was first detected as a sense by a perceptographer in the Senses Bureau.

THERE IS A RAPIDLY GROWING SENSE THAT THE PRESIDENT IS PURSUING A DANGEROUS POLICY WITH REGARD TO NUCLEAR ARMS.

Immediately Perceiver General Hotwall was notified.

LOOKS LIKE TROUBLE...WE'VE GOT TO DIFFUSE IT BEFORE IT BECOMES A PERCEPTION!

BZZZN...

PERCEPT

UH-OH!

IT JUST DID.

As his staff swung into action, tracking and charting the new perception, Hotwall began giving orders.

GET ME THE WHITE HOUSE...and the OFFICE OF LIP SERVICE!...

The next day he met with the President and told him of the perception.

HOW BAD IS IT, BAYARD? COULD IT DAMAGE MY PRESTIGE?

WELL...IT'S SERIOUS, BUT I THINK we can NEUTRALIZE IT. I'VE GOT SOME IDEAS...

Later that week the President gave his first address to the nation on the subject of nuclear disarmament:

WE MUST ESTABLISH A DIALOGUE WITH THE SOVIETS.

FOR THIS PURPOSE, I WILL APPOINT A TEAM OF OUR FINEST METEOROLOGISTS to MEET *in* GENEVA WITH tHEIR SOVIET COUNTER-PARTS *and* BEGIN COMPREHENSIVE DISCUSSIONS OF tHE WEATHER.

WE WILL CALL tHESE TALKS **STALL** -STRATEGIC ARMS LIMITATION LIMBO.

THE **STALL** TALKS WILL CONTINUE UNTIL WE WIN THE ARMS RACE, AT WHICH TIME WE WILL APPOINT A TEAM OF INTERIOR DESIGNERS to BEGIN NEGOTIATIONS ON THE SHAPE OF THE BARGAINING TABLE.

DURING THE WEEKS THAT FOLLOWED, BAYARD KEPT A CLOSE WATCH ON THE UNWANTED PERCEPTION

HAS IT DIMINISHED YET?

NOT MUCH.

NOT AS MUCH, FOR INSTANCE, AS A CERTAIN PERCEPTION OF BOB FOREHEAD.

HE KNOWS A LOT MORE THAN I THOUGHT HE DID!

IT ALL BEGAN OVER A BOWL OF CEREAL...
A MAJOR SHIFT in the POLITICAL DIRECTION OF A FUTURE DAY AMERICA.

© 1982 m.a.8

WHEN I GROW UP, I'M GONNA BE A FIREMAN!

I'M GONNA BE A DOCTOR. WHAT ARE YOU GONNA BE, ROGER?

I'M GONNA BE A SEND-AWAYER.

A WHAT?!!

ROGER DIDN'T KNOW HOW TO EXPLAIN IT. HE WASN'T EVEN SURE IF THERE WERE SUCH A JOB. BUT IF THERE WEREN'T, HE THOUGHT HE MIGHT INVENT IT...

...BECAUSE SENDING away FOR THINGS WAS HIS FAVORITE THING TO DO.

HEY, MOM! LOOK! MY PLASTIC MOTH JUST CAME IN THE MAIL!

the ANTICIPATION... the NERVOUS EXCITEMENT... IT THRILLED HIM LIKE NOTHING ELSE COULD.

AS HE WAS GROWING UP, ROGER SENT AWAY FOR all SORTS OF things... THROUGH CEREAL BOXES, ADS in COMIC BOOKS, mail ORDER CATALOGUES, etcetera.

ONE DAY HE RECEIVED a CHAIN LETTER. HE mailed one DOLLAR to EACH OF 10 PEOPLE. THREE WEEKS LATER he RECEIVED $973 in 973 ENVELOPES.

WOW! I CAN even SEND AWAY FOR MONEY!!

IN COLLEGE, HE HAD A ROOMMATE WITH STRONG POLITICAL IDEAS.

THE SECULAR HUMANIST LIBERALS ARE DESTROYING AMERICA!

OVER time, ROGER GOT CONVINCED..

At HIS ROOMMATE'S URGING, HE JOINED A RADICAL ORGANIZATION called tHE CONSERVATIVE LIBERATION FRONT, SHOWN HERE WEARING THEIR EMBLEM: tHE STRIPED NECKtIE HEADBAND.

WHEN tHE CLF NEEDED MONEY, ROGER HAD A SOLUTION.

I'LL SEND OUT A CHAIN LETTER.

IN tHE years tHAT FOLLOWED, ROGER SENT OUT LOTS OF CHAIN LETTERS and RAISED LOTS OF MONEY. He also BUILT UP a mailing LIST FOR DIRECT MAIL SOLICITATION, tHE BIGGEST MAILING LIST in HISTORY.

All DAY LONG ROGER WROTE and MAILED LETTERS, asking PEOPLE for MONEY.

WHEN HIS FORMER ROOMMATE, CLANCY FUMES, RAN FOR tHE U.S. SENATE, ROGER PAID tHE WAY.

In tHE years FOLLOWING CLANCY'S ELECTION, HE and ROGER SET to WORK REMAKING AMERICA.

I tHINK tHAT GUY FOREHEAD COULD HELP US.

MAYBE SO. IF HE'S NOT TOO FLAKEY.

IT WAS A PERFECT DAY FOR GOLF, BUT GERARD OXBOGGLE WAS DISTRACTED.

IS SOMETHING BOTHERING YOU, SIR?

HIS GUEST FOR THE DAY WAS CONGRESSMAN BOB FOREHEAD.

NO, NOTHING... NOTHING.

IT'S NO USE!

I CAN'T CONCEN-TRATE...

I CAN'T PLAY GOLF NOW...IT JUST KEEPS CROSSING MY MIND...

WHAT IS IT, SIR?

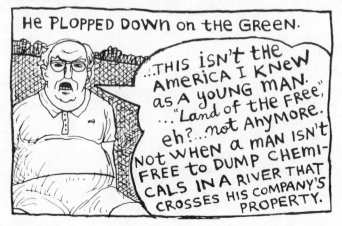

HE PLOPPED DOWN ON THE GREEN.

...THIS ISN'T THE AMERICA I KNEW AS A YOUNG MAN. ..."LAND OF THE FREE," EH?...NOT ANYMORE. NOT WHEN A MAN ISN'T FREE TO DUMP CHEMI-CALS IN A RIVER THAT CROSSES HIS COMPANY'S PROPERTY.

THOSE ECOLOGY FREAKS... THEY THINK THEY'RE SO "IN TOUCH" WITH NATURE. THEY WANT ME TO BUILD ALL SORTS OF COSTLY CONTRAPTIONS FOR DISPOSAL OF CHEMICAL WASTE DESPITE THE FACT THAT NATURE HAS ALREADY PROVIDED A RIVER THAT IS PERFECT FOR THE JOB.

IT'S MADNESS! ...FOR A WHILE I COULD TAKE IT... THE ANNOYANCE, THE ANXIETY... BUT NOW THAT IT'S BEGUN TO AFFECT MY GOLF GAME...

...IT'S GONE TOO FAR!

THE PAINED EXPRESSION ON MR. OXBOGGLE'S FACE HAUNTED BOB FOREHEAD FOR DAYS.

HE TALKED OVER THE PROBLEM WITH HIS STAFF.

I'VE GOT AN IDEA!

SAID CHIP CHAPWOOD, A BRIGHT, YOUNG AIDE.

TWO WEEKS LATER BOB WENT TO THE FLOOR OF THE HOUSE TO INTRODUCE H.R. 7571569395186,

...THE DUMPING RIGHTS ACT OF 1982...

THEN HE MET WITH HIS CAUCUS...

BOB FOREHEAD'S EYES WERE VERY MOIST.

It WAS A TERRIBLE THING to witness. MR. OXBOGGLE JUST STOOD THERE, his GOLF CLUB TREMBLING in his hands... UNABLE to CONCENTRATE on the GAME...

...UNABLE to GET HIS mind OFF OF THE TERRIBLE FRUSTRATION he FEELS OVER GOVERNMENT IMPINGEMENT ON HIS RIGHT to DUMP CHEMICALS. THE man is SUFFERING AN INCREDIBLE ANXIETY.

...WHICH is PART OF THE HUMAN COST OF BIG GOVERNMENT, the SORT OF THING THAT LIBERALS AVOID MENTIONING...

THUS did BOB MAKE HIS PLEA to THE JFK-LOOK-ALIKE CAUCUS to SUPPORT HIS DUMPING RIGHTS ACT.

The FOLLOWING WEEK HEARINGS BEGAN BEFORE the HOUSE MISCELLANY COMMITTEE SUBCOMMITTEE on FISHING RODS, HOME APPLIANCES and CHEMICAL WASTE to STUDY THE BILL'S MERITS.

FROM HIS SEAT ON THAT SUBCOMMITTEE, BOB PERFORMED WELL.

THE KID'S GOT TALENT.

OBSERVED SENATOR CLANCY FUMES.

WE'LL SEE...

ONE DAY SENATOR FUMES HAD LUNCH WITH CONGRESSMAN FOREHEAD.

HOW'D YOU LIKE TO EXPAND YOUR CONSTITUENCY ...nationwide?

I... I'D LIKE THAT.

I HAVE ACCESS to SEVERAL LARGE MAILING LISTS THROUGH VARIOUS ORGANIZATIONS WITH WHICH I AM AFFILIATED.

THESE ORGANIZATIONS ARE CONCERNED ABOUT MORAL DECAY. THEY WOULD LOOK FAVORABLY UPON YOUR SUPPORT OF MY BILL TO ESTABLISH A FEDERAL OFFICE OF PERSONAL LIFE MANAGEMENT.

HOW ABOUT IT?

AT THAT POINT, BOB UTTERED A SOUND THAT SOUNDED AFFIRMATIVE, BUT MIGHT NOT HAVE BEEN, BUT MIGHT HAVE BEEN, BUT MIGHT NOT HAVE BEEN, BUT MIGHT HAVE BEEN, BUT MIGHT NOT HAVE BEEN, BUT MIGHT HAVE BEEN, BUT MIGHT NOT HAVE BEEN, BUT

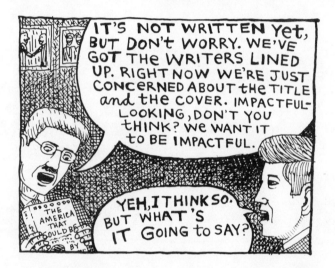

JUST THEN AN AIDE came IN.

SENATOR FUMES **CALLED. HE'LL** PICK YOU UP *in* 10 MINUTES.

SENATOR FUMES DROVE BOB TO THE airport and they caught A PLANE SOUTH to the SENATOR'S HOMETOWN.

I WANTED YOU TO SEE THIS FOR YOURSELF. I'VE GOT A DEDICATED BUNCH HERE.

THE CLANCY FUMES COLLEGE OF MORALITY MANAGEMENT

THEY WENT OUT BACK and WATCHED THE CHAPERONE SQUADS PERFORMING THEIR AFTERNOON DRILLS.

SUCH PRECISION!

THEY'RE THE BEST!

THE NEXT DAY BOB EMBARKED ON A BRIEF SPEAKING TOUR to TEST HIS FUZZWORDS in VARIOUS PARTS OF THE COUNTRY.

AS BOB FLEW FROM CITY TO CITY AROUND THE nation, ANOTHER PERSON WAS WALKING FROM HOUSE to HOUSE in BOB'S HOME DISTRICT.

HELLO. MY NAME IS ALLEN SOUP. I'm RUNNING FOR CONGRESS.

...I'm NOT A MEDIA IMAGE. I'm NOT SOME CAREFULLY PACKAGED PRODUCT. I'm A FLESH and BLOOD **PERSON** WHO LIVES in THIS AREA and CARES ABOUT IT.

IN 23 YEARS OF SERVICE to OUR COMMUNITY, FIRST AS A GAS METER READER and THEN AS AN ENCYCLOPEDIA SALESMAN, I'VE TRAVELED ALL OVER THIS CONGRESSIONAL DISTRICT. I KNOW ITS PEOPLE and THEIR PROBLEMS, PEOPLE like YOURSELVES, MR. and MRS. GLACKLINGER. I SHARE YOUR CONCERNS.

NOW TELL ME SOME-THING:

WHEN WAS THE LAST TIME THAT BOB FOREHEAD SAT WITH *you* in YOUR LIVING ROOM LIKE THIS AND LISTENED to YOUR IDEAS?

MR. and MRS. GLACKLINGER THOUGHT.

...NEVER.

NO, NEVER.

I GUESS HE'S JUST too BUSY WITH HIS WASHINGTON GLAMOUR-BOY LIFE and HIS JETSETTING around THE COUNTRY. I THINK HE'S LOST TOUCH WITH US, WITH **THE PEOPLE.**

maybe so...

ALLEN SOUP'S CANDIDACY GOT A SLOW START. SO SLOW THAT BOB FOREHEAD'S STAFF DID NOT, AT FIRST, TAKE NOTICE OF an EVER-SO-GRADUAL EROSION OF BOB'S initial POWER BASE.

I LIKE HIM.

maybe we need a change

THEY, AFTER ALL, were casting THEIR gaze on GRANDER HORIZONS as BOB HOPPED FROM CITY TO CITY, DAZZLING AUDIENCES with charm and FUZZWORDS.

meanwhile, BACK in WASHINGTON, REPORTER malcolm FRAZZLE was DISCUSSING WITH A COLLEAGUE something HE'D BEEN TOLD BY A DRUNKEN FACTORY WORKER from the GLOMINOID CORPORATION.

HE SAID HE WAS BEING TRANSFERRED TO THEIR WEAPONS DIVISION TO WORK ON A NEW PROJECT...

...the DEVELOPMENT OF A BOMB THAT KILLS ONLY THOSE PEOPLE WHO DON'T carry CREDIT CARDS. HE SAID IT'S TOP SECRET.

"TOP SECRET" OR NOT, SEVERAL UNAUTHORIZED PEOPLE KNEW OF the PROJECT.

I WANT THAT BOMB!

GOOD AFTERNOON, SIR. IS THE MINISTER OF DEFENSE IN?

I'LL SEE.

A FEW minutes LATER an INTENSE-LOOKING MAN APPEARED at the GOVERNMENT PALACE DOOR.

YOU WISH to SEE ME?

YESSIR. GOOD AFTERNOON. I'm YOUR GLOMINOID CORPORATION DIVISION OF WEAPONRY PERSONAL REPRESENTATIVE. I HAVE A FREE GIFT and I'D LIKE to SHOW you SOME of the other items THAT WE CARRY.

THE FREE GIFT WAS A WARHEAD FOR A SHORT-RANGE SURFACE-to-AIR missile. THE DEFENSE minister APPEARED PLEASED.

COME IN.

They ENTERED A LARGE ROOM and SAT DOWN ON A COUCH. THE SALESMAN OPENED HIS CATALOGUE.

WE HAVE A SPECIAL OFFER this month ONLY: FOR EVERY half dozen ANTI-AIRCRAFT GUNS THAT YOU BUY, YOU'LL RECEIVE, FREE OF CHARGE, ONE 500-POUND DEMOLITION BOMB... WHILE THEY LAST.

THE DEFENSE minister seemed DISTRACTED. HE FLIPPED ahead THROUGH THE CATALOGUE.

THESE POP GUNS and LITTLE BOMBS ARE all VERY CUTE, BUT WE'VE GOT PLENTY RIGHT NOW.

WE may BE a SMALL nation, BUT WE'RE NOT CHILDREN... IT'S time WE WERE TREATED LiKE ADULTS.

WHAT DO YOU MEAN?

I MEAN, HOW ABOUT SOME NUKES?!

WELL, I DON'T THINK CONGRESS WOULD APPROVE...

WE'RE PREPARED TO FUND A FULL-SCALE LOBBYING EFFORT...

Well, I just DON'T THINK ... NOT NOW ... NOT in THE PRESENT POLITICAL climate

AFTER THE SALESMAN LEFT, THE DEFENSE MINISTER PAID A VISIT to HIS nation's LEADER, COLONEL ANNOYU.

...HE DOESN'T THINK IT WOULD GET THROUGH CONGRESS. DON'T WORRY...

...THERE ARE OTHER WAYS. ... THERE ARE OTHER WAYS...

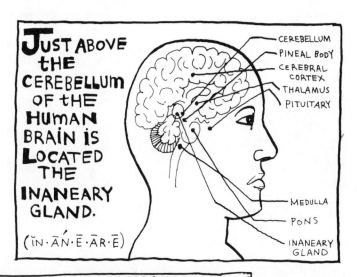

JUST ABOVE tHE CEREBELLUM OF THE HUMAN BRAIN iS LOCATED THE INANEARY GLAND.

(ĬN·ĀŃ·Ē·ĀR·Ē)

CEREBELLUM
PINEAL BODY
CEREBRAL CORTEX
THALAMUS
PITUITARY

MEDULLA
PONS
INANEARY GLAND

The FUNCTION OF THIS GLAND IS THE SECRETION OF A FLUID WHICH AIDS the BRAIN in THE GENERATION OF SMALL TALK.

SO HOW IS YOUR FAMILY?

ARE YOU SPEAKING in A SPIRITUAL, METABOLIC, OR HISTORICAL CONTEXT?

PERSON WITH A HEALTHY INANEARY GLAND

VICTIM OF INANEARY MALFUNCTION

WHILE THERE ARE VARIOUS TYPES OF INANEARY DISORDERS AFFLICTING LARGE SEGMENTS OF OUR POPULATION, MOST VICTIMS CAN LIVE RELATIVELY UNTROUBLED LIVES.

HUH?

WHAT?

FOR PEOPLE in CERTAIN PROFESSIONS, HOWEVER, WHICH REQUIRE FREQUENT ATTENDANCE at COCKTAIL PARTIES, the STRAIN ON THIS GLAND IS SOMETIMES OVERWHELMING and A MALFUNCTION COULD ENDANGER A CAREER.

THAT'S WHY MODERN SCIENCE INVENTED "PALAVERZINE", A MEDICATION IN PILL FORM.

PALAVERZINE

DON'T TAKE TOO MANY, BOB.

I'VE GOT SIX COCKTAIL PARTIES TONIGHT.

SAID CONGRESS-MAN BOB FOREHEAD.

I'LL NEVER GET THROUGH IT...

BOB GOT THROUGH THE NIGHT ALL RIGHT and CHATTED UNTIL THE NEXT MORNING.

GREAT TO SEE YOU...

NO PARKING

THEN HE ATTENDED A BREAKFAST AT THE "PLUTONIUM CLUB" AND HEARD SOME PASSIONATE SPEECHES.

WE'VE GOT TO STRAIGHTEN OUT PUBLIC THINKING ON THIS ISSUE OF NUCLEAR PROLIFERATION. MOST PEOPLE ARE AFRAID OF IT...

...WHEN, IN FACT, IT IS OUR ONLY HOPE.

ONLY WHEN EVERY NATION HAS THE ABILITY TO BLOW ITS NEIGHBOR OFF THE FACE OF THE EARTH WILL WE HAVE THE SORT OF BALANCE THAT EQUALS TRUE PEACE AND STABILITY.

PEACE THROUGH PROLIFERATIVE PARITY

THAT DINETTE SET STOOD THERE BURNING ITS *IMAGE* into RALPH'S MIND.

THAT WOULD LOOK SO NICE WITH OUR DRAPES.

RALPH'S FACE BECAME SUDDENLY TENSE.

WE CAN'T AFFORD IT. WE OWE TOO MUCH ALREADY.

he SAID, THE WORDS STICKING in HIS THROAT!

LOOK at THOSE COUCHES!...

LET'S GET OUT OF HERE!

MAYBE IT WAS NOTHING MORE THAN SOCIAL CONDITIONING, BUT IT FUNCTIONED IN RALPH LIKE A PRIMORDIAL INSTINCT, HIS DRIVE TO CONSUME MERCHANDISE.

I WORK HARD FOR MY MONEY...

HE SAID to A FRIEND in A TAVERN the NEXT EVENING.

...I SHOULD BE ABLE to AFFORD A NEW DINETTE SET IF I WANT ONE... and A NEW CAR... and A NEW HOUSE...

AS RALPH CONTINUED TALKING, NEITHER HE NOR HIS FRIEND NOTICED THE MUSSY-HAIRED MAN WHO STOOD QUIETLY BEHIND THEIR BOOTH, LISTENING CLOSELY TO EVERY WORD.

...I need MORE MONEY...

THE NEXT DAY AT HIS JOB ASSEMBLING HIGH-TECHNOLOGY DEVICES in THE WEAPONS DIVISION OF THE GLOMINOID CORPORATION, RALPH COULD NOT GET THE DINETTE SET OFF HIS MIND.

SEVERAL DAYS LATER RALPH MADE THE AQUAINTANCE OF A MUSSY-HAIRED MAN WHO HAPPENED TO SIT BESIDE HIM ON A STOOL in THE TAVERN.

YOU LOOK TROUBLED

EVENTUALLY RALPH GOT AROUND TO COMPLAINING ABOUT HIS SALARY.

I'm in HOCK UP TO MY MUSTACHE.

THE STRANGER OFFERED A SUGGESTION.

IF ONE OF THOSE DEVICES YOU ASSEMBLE WERE TO FIND ITS WAY INTO MY HANDS, A LARGE SUM OF MONEY WOULD FIND ITS WAY INTO YOURS.

RALPH HAD TO THINK ABOUT THAT...

ONE SATURDAY RALPH TOLD HIS WIFE HE WAS TAKING THE CAR TO A MECHANIC for a TUNE-UP.

INSTEAD, HOWEVER, HE DROVE to THE SHOPPING MALL for ANOTHER LOOK at the DINETTE SET WHOSE PRICE EXCEEDED HIS PURCHASING POWER.

FOR SEVERAL HOURS RALPH STOOD THERE, IGNORING SALES CLERKS, OBLIVIOUS to the WORLD. THIS DINETTE SET HAD BECOME MORE to HIM THAN MERE FURNITURE...

...IT WAS HIS MT. MCKINLEY, HIS MOBY DICK... A CHALLENGE to HIS PERSONAL ESTEEM... And IT WAS GETTING THE BETTER OF HIM.

EXCUSE ME, SIR. WE'RE CLOSING.

HE MUST HAVE STOOD BY THAT PHONE BOOTH FOR MORE THAN AN HOUR, PACING, muttering, leaving and RETURNing.

PHONE

Finally HE MADE the CALL.

HELLO... THIS IS RALPH. ...I'M READY to DO BUSINESS.

IT TOOK THE BETTER PART OF two *months*, PIECE BY PIECE, to GET THE TOP SECRET "HIGH-TECH" DEVICE PAST FACTORY SECURITY and SLOWLY REASSEMBLE *it* IN HIS BASEMENT.

TWO DAYS AFTER IT WAS DELIVERED TO a CERTAIN MUSSY-HAIRED *man*, RALPH FOUND HIMSELF IN A POSITION to PURCHASE THE *Dinette* SET. ... and A NEW CAR.

RALPH ENJOYED HIS NEW POSSESSIONS IMMENSELY, BUT THEY DID NOT QUELL HIS APPETITE FOR MORE.

WE REALLY DO NEED A NEW HOUSE.

THE MUSSY-HAIRED MAN DERIVED GREAT BENEFIT FROM THE DEVICE THAT RALPH HAD GIVEN HIM...

EXCELLENT WORK!

BUT HIS APPETITE WAS NOT QUELLED EITHER.

NEITHER WAS THAT OF HIS BOSS.

DOES HE HAVE ACCESS TO ANY PART OF THAT BOMB?

I'M NOT SURE YET, BUT I'LL FIND OUT.

FORTUNATELY FOR THE MORGELSON FAMILY, SEVERAL SHIPMENTS OF WASHINGTON D.C. SOUVENIR THERMOMETERS HAD ARRIVED THAT VERY MORNING FROM HONG KONG.

AIR HONG KONG

JIMMY WAS VERY EXCITED TO RECEIVE HIS OFFICIAL SOUVENIR OF WASHINGTON D.C.

WOW!

MADE IN HONGKONG

...and HE WAS VERY UPSET A WEEK LATER BACK HOME in KANSAS WHEN HE REALIZED HE'D LEFT HIS SOUVENIR IN THE HOTEL.

I WANT MY THERMOMETER!

HIS PARENTS FELT BAD TOO, LOOKING INTO HIS SAD, YOUNG EYES, and FEELING HIS SENSE OF LOSS.

...WHICH IS HOW BOB FOREHEAD FELT, LOOKING into GERARD OXBOGGLE'S EYES THAT SAME NIGHT in A RESTAURANT BACK in WASHINGTON.

I WANT MY TAX BREAKS!

I'M TRYING TO SAVE THEM, BUT WE DON'T SEEM TO HAVE enough VOTES.

THEY WOULDN'T BE DOING THIS IF **YOU** WERE PRESIDENT!

SAID MR. OXBOGGLE.

BOB FOREHEAD LIKED the SOUND OF THAT,

...AND THOUGHT ABOUT IT OFTEN AS HE TRAVELED TO VARIOUS PARTS OF THE COUNTRY FOR HIS HEAVY SCHEDULE OF SPEAKING ENGAGEMENTS.

ONE PLACE HE HADN'T VISITED RECENTLY, HOWEVER, WAS HIS HOME DISTRICT.

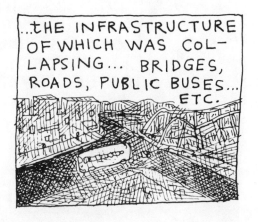

...THE INFRASTRUCTURE OF WHICH WAS COLLAPSING... BRIDGES, ROADS, PUBLIC BUSES... ETC.

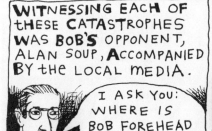

WITNESSING EACH OF THESE CATASTROPHES WAS BOB'S OPPONENT, ALAN SOUP, ACCOMPANIED BY THE LOCAL MEDIA.

I ASK YOU: WHERE IS BOB FOREHEAD NOW?

BACK in WASHINGTON ANOTHER PERSON WAS ASKING THAT SAME QUESTION WITH increasing FREQUENCY.

WHERE IS HE?

THIS OTHER PERSON WAS BOB'S WIFE, GINGER.

WITH THAT, HE HANDED HER A PENCIL and PAPER and RAN OUT THE DOOR.

I'M LATE!

Ginger MADE A FEW SKETCHES, BUT SOON GOT BORED. Sitting ALONE on a FRIDAY NIGHT SKETCHING MISSILE-BASING SYSTEMS WAS NOT HER IDEA OF A GOOD time.

THEN THE OTHER SIDE OF GINGER FOREHEAD BEGAN TO EMERGE... the SIDE that BOB KNEW VERY LITTLE ABOUT...

SHE WENT TO HER CLOSET and PULLED OUT HER SECRET OUTFIT. and PUT IT ON.

HALF an hour LATER SHE ARRIVED at THE DISCO. A PUNK BAND WAS PLAYING. THE MUSIC GRAB-BED HER.

AFTER A WHILE, A CERTAIN MUSSY-HAIRED MAN ASKED HER TO DANCE. GINGER FOUND IT SOMEHOW STRANGELY EXCITING TO DANCE WITH A MAN WHO DIDN'T USE A BLOWDRYER, OR A COMB.

AS THEY DANCED, AN ASSEMBLER OF HI-TECH EQUIPMENT named RALPH WAS TRYING to REACH THE MAN BY PHONE.

NUTS! HE'S NOT HOME!

WHAT'S YOUR NAME? Said the mussy-haired man.

UH... SHEILA. SAID GINGER FOREHEAD.

IT WAS THE FIRST NAME THAT POPPED into HER MIND.

CAN I CALL YOU?

...um, well... I DON'T have A PHONE... I-I'M JUST VISITING. ...THANK YOU...UH, GOOD NIGHT.

SO THAT WAS THAT: A NIGHT AT THE DISCO. LET OFF A LITTLE STEAM. THEN GO BACK TO HER NORMAL LIFE. VERY SIMPLE.

...OR WAS IT?

...WHY DID THE IMAGE OF THE MUSSY-HAIRED MAN LINGER IN HER MIND?

WHY DID SHE SUDDENLY FEEL SO IRRITATED EACH MORNING BY THE SOUND OF HER HUSBAND'S BLOWDRYER?

SOMETHING ABOUT THE MUSSY-HAIRED MAN EXCITED HER, INTRIGUED HER.

THIS IS CRAZY! ...I THINK I HAVE A CRUSH ON HIM.

DID YOU SAY SOMETHING, GINGER?

HUH? ...UH, NO...NO. JUST TALKING TO MYSELF.

...I wonder WHERE HE IS NOW... I WONDER WHAT HE'S DOING...

I'M LATE AGAIN, BUT WE'LL TALK SOON, GINGER. I PROMISE... SOMETIME AFTER NOVEMBER. OR NEXT YEAR!

FOR several minutes GINGER SAT THERE, making WILD GUESSES ABOUT the IDENTITY OF the STRANGER.

maybE HE'S A musician ...OR A FiLM DIRECTOR ...OR A...

ONE thing SHE DIDN'T GUESS WAS that HE miGHT BE A DEFENSE miNiSTER FOR A SMALL, VOLAtiLE NATiON,...

Hello, Ralph.

...ACTIVELY ENGAGED in the ILLEGAL ACQUISITION OF TOP SECRET U.S. MILITARY DEVICES.

...MY WiFE WANTS to REDO OUR DINING ROOM and KITCHEN to GO WITH OUR NEW DiNettE SET. IT DOESN'T GO WITH THE DRAPES AFTER ALL...

FINE, FINE...

...I've HEARD ABOUT A NEW POCKET-SIZE ANTi-PERSONNEL DEViCE tHAT AttACHES to A PORTABLE TAPE-PLAYER. Can you GEt me SOME?

SURE.

WE'RE LOOKING DOWN the ROAD at A DAY WHEN GLOMinoid WILL PRODUCE A LINE OF PORTABLE WAR CASSETTES capable OF CONDUCTING an ENTIRE LIMITED-SCALE WAR free OF HUMAN INTERVENTION.

Said THE SALES REPRESENTATIVE FOR THE GLOMINOID CORPORATION DIVISION OF WEAPONRY.

...YOU'LL SIMPLY PLUG the CASSETTE into the COMMAND CONTROL OF any COMPATIBLE WEAPONS SYSTEM, SIT BACK, RELAX, and WATCH YOUR WAR VIA SATELLITE... OR "DALLAS" IF YOU PREFER...

THE DEFENSE MINISTER OF the SMALL NATION OF FANATISTAN LISTENED carefully.

FOR THE PRESENT, however, you MIGHT BE interested to KNOW that I JUST MADE A BIG SALE to YOUR NEIGHBOR to the WEST, TYRANIA.

THE FANATISTANIAN DEFENSE MINISTER'S EYES DARKENED.

ONE DAY SENATOR FUMES MET WITH DIRECT MAIL SPECIALIST ROBERT VINEGAR to DISCUSS THE UPCOMING *Congressional* ELECTIONS.

WE'VE GOT to STOP THOSE BIG SPENDERS ...*no* MATTER **HOW** MUCH it COSTS!

MEANWHILE, ALLEN SOUP, the UNDER-FUNDED *challenger* to CONGRESSMAN BOB FOREHEAD, WAS TRYING *to* MAKE the *most* OF HIS *limited* FUNDS.

YOU PROBABLY WON'T SEE *this* T.V. SPOT VERY OFTEN. I DON'T *have* ACCESS to the KIND OF MONEY MY OPPONENT DOES. SO I HOPE YOU'LL LISTEN CLOSELY to WHAT I SAY...

...I'M NOT A **GLAMOUR-BOY** LIKE BOB FORE-HEAD *with* WEALTHY *contributors* PAY-ING BIG MONEY *to* MOLD *my* "IMAGE"...

...WHAT I AM IS **A REGULAR PERSON**, LIKE MANY OF YOU, CONCERNED ABOUT *the* DETERIORATION OF OUR LOCAL COMMUNITIES *and* WONDERING WHAT BOB FOREHEAD IS DOING ABOUT IT..

...Well, I'LL **TELL** YOU WHAT HE'S DOING: HE'S RUNNING ALL OVER THE COUNTRY MAKING SPEECHES, PURSUING HIS OWN PERSONAL AMBITIONS. HE'S OUT OF TOUCH WITH THE PEOPLE WHO ELECTED HIM!

...I SAY IT'S TIME TO SEND A **REGULAR PERSON** TO WASHINGTON TO SHAKE UP *the* BIG SHOTS *and* SPEAK FOR THE *needs* OF **THE PEOPLE!**

ALLEN SOUP'S MEDIA ADVISERS **ALL** AGREED THAT THIS "REGULAR **PERSON**" ANTI-IMAGE IMAGE WAS THE BEST IMAGE FOR ALLEN TO ADOPT.

...and OPINION POLLS BEGAN TO PROVE THEY WERE RIGHT.

RE-ELECT BOB FOREHEAD
RE-ELECT BOB FOREHEAD
RE-ELECT F...
RE-ELECT BOB FOREHEAD

I TELL YOU THIS GUY SOUP IS HURTING US! WE'VE GOT TO GET BOB TO MAKE SOME LOCAL APPEARANCES!

NOT THIS WEEK. HE'S IN TEXAS.

MEANWHILE, ALLEN SOUP *took* HIS FAMILY TO A COMMUNITY CENTER PICNIC, ...

HEE HEE HEE!

HOW ADORABLE!
WHAT A NICE FAMILY!

...and GOT THEIR PICTURE IN ALL THE LOCAL PAPERS.

The Fog Township Courier
LIFE SECTION
700 ATTEND ANNUAL PICNIC
THE SNEEZE COUNTY RECORD
THE ITCHVILLE GAZETTE

WHEREUPON, the assistant MANAGER OF BOB'S RE-ELECTION CAMPAIGN PLACED A CALL TO **Him** in DALLAS, TEXAS.

RE-ELECT BOB FOREHEAD

...YOU'VE GOT TO GET BACK HERE TO THE HOME DISTRICT NEXT WEEKEND, BOB. ...AND **BRING YOUR FAMILY!**

That NIGHT BOB called HIS WIFE, GINGER, in WASHINGTON. THERE WAS NO ANSWER. HE TRIED SEVERAL TIMES.

Finally, at 4:30 A.m., he REACHED her.

WHERE WERE YOU?

OUT. SHE SAID.

THERE WAS A STRANGE TONE TO HER VOICE. SHE SOUNDED LIKE A DIFFERENT PERSON.

?

THE NEXT DAY:

INSTEAD OF REMODELING OUR DINING ROOM and KITCHEN, MY WIFE and I have DECIDED WE WANT A NEW HOUSE.

SAID Ralph to the MUSSY-HAIRED man.

YOU'LL **HAVE** A NEW HOUSE... A MANSION. ...IF YOU Can PROVIDE me with A certain BOMB I'VE HEARD ABOUT...

...A BOMB THAT KILLS only THOSE PEOPLE who don't CARRY CREDiT CARDS.

I... I DON'T WORK in THAT SECTION, BUT I'LL SEE WHAT I can DO.

I want THAT BOMB **NOW!** SAID Colonel Annoyu when his DEFENSE minister REPORTED BACK to HIM.

IF GINGER FOREHEAD HAD made A list of all THE PLACES SHE WOULD HAVE LIKED to have been on THAT SATURDAY AFTERNOON, the DEDICATION ceremony FOR the GRAND OPENING of the SMOGHURST SHOPPING MALL would not HAVE BEEN HIGH ON HER LIST.

WE are GATHERED here today Not MERELY to DEDICATE A SHOPPING MALL, BUT to REDEDICATE OUR-SELVES, MIND and BODY, to the SPIRIT of CONSUMERISM, and to SEEK AN EVER MORE DEEPLY-INDEBTED RELATIONSHIP to tHe PROCESS of PURCHASING MERCHANDISE...

AT the URGING OF HER HUSBAND'S CAMPAIGN MANAGER, HOWEVER, GINGER DUTIFULLY attended, ...Not with out DIS-COM-FORt.

DURING THE BAND CONCERT, she BEGAN to FEEL a KNOT,... TWISTING EVER tiGHTER in THE PIT OF her STOMACH.

LATER THEY went to BOB'S campaign HEADQUARTERS, WHERE AN ARGUMENT had BROKEN OUT Between BOB'S CHIEF PERCEPTUAL ENGINEER and HIS CHARISMATICIAN OVER the LENGTH OF their candidate's SIDEBURNS.

That EVENING BOB and GINGER Returned to WASHINGTON.

EXHAUSTED FROM RECENT TRAVELS, BOB FELL ASLEEP RIGHT AWAY.

GINGER COULDN'T SLEEP.

IT WAS 12:30 A.M. WHEN SHE FINALLY tip-toED to HeR CLOSEt, PUT ON HER SECRET OUTFIT. and SET OUT FOR tHE DISCO.

SHE'D BEEN DANCING ALONE FOR 20 min-utes WHEN SHE HEARD a FAMILIAR VOICE.

HELLO, SHEILA.

...HUH?

YOUR namE IS SHEILA, ISN'T IT?

...OH, UH, ...YES...YES. ...UH, Hi...

THEY DANCED and DANCED...

meanwhile, BOB FOREHEAD WOKE UP.

...GINGER? ...GINGER?

...WHERE IS SHE?!

2:25 A.M. at the DISCO!

WHY DON'T WE GO OUT FOR A NIGHT-CAP, SHEILA?

said the mussy-haired MAN.

OH, UH, ...O.K.

said GINGER FORE-HEAD.

THEY DROVE in HIS CAR.

I JUST HAVE TO STOP AT my BANK and GET some MONEY... I'LL BE A FEW minutes.

24 HOUR BANKING

O.K.

AS SHE WAITED BESIDE the *car*, GINGER NOTICED SOMETHING on the BACK SEAT.

A PORTABLE RADIO/CASSETTE PLAYER!

SHE *took* IT OUT and SET IT DOWN on the *hood* OF the CAR.

I'VE NEVER SEEN SUCH A FANCY one BEFORE!

SHE TURNED on some MUSIC.

GEE, I WONDER WHAT THIS GADGET DOES.

NOT BEING FAMILIAR with TOP-SECRET WEAPONS TECHNOLOGY, GINGER DID NOT REALIZE THAT the "GADGET" WAS A CRAMM, (CLOSE-RANGE AUTOMATIC MESS-MAKER).

...IT MUST BE SOME SORT OF AMP'...

...I WONDER HOW YOU TURN IT ON...

...I'D LIKE **EACH** OF YOU TO ASK YOURSELF A QUESTION: ... **WHAT** HAS BOB FOREHEAD DONE FOR **YOU**?!

said ALLEN SOUP, *the challenger.*

...HAS HE IMPROVED THE QUALITY OF *your* **LIFE**? HAS HE MADE YOU A **HAPPIER PERSON**?...

IN HIS **FOUR YEARS** *in* THE **MOST POWERFUL LEGISLATIVE BODY** *in* THE **WORLD**, HAVE YOU **FELT** THAT **AWESOME POWER** WORKING FOR **YOU**?!

HE WAS **SEEING IT** MORE *and* MORE NOW,.. ...a CERTAIN *look* IN THE **VOTERS'** *eyes*...

...*not* UNLIKE THE **LOOK** *he'd* SEEN *in* CUSTOMERS' EYES *in* TWELVE YEARS AS *an* ENCYCLOPEDIA SALESMAN.

...THIS COULD VERY WELL BE THE MOST IMPORTANT PURCHASE YOU WILL EVER MAKE ...FOR YOURSELF, FOR YOUR CHILDREN, FOR GENERATIONS *to* COME...

THE ENCYCLOPEDIA BALONEYA

HE ALWAYS SAW IT JUST BEFORE HE MADE A SALE.

MAYBE YOU'RE RIGHT...

...*and* HE WAS SEEING *it*, WITH *increasing* FREQUENCY *now*, AMONG *the* VOTERS.

...THIS *may* VERY WELL BE *the* MOST IMPORTANT VOTE YOU WILL EVER CAST... FOR YOURSELF, FOR YOUR CHILDREN, FOR GENERATIONS *to* COME...

Meanwhile, BOB FOREHEAD'S CAMPAIGN WAS PLAGUED WITH internal STRIFE.

LISTEN, BOB, WE'RE in TROUBLE. YOU'VE GOT to START USING MORE BUZZWORDS! SAID HIS CHARISMATICIAN.

RE-ELECT BOB FOREHEAD

DON'T LISTEN to HIM, BOB! SAID HIS PERCEPTUAL ENGINEER.

THE FOLLOWING NIGHT THE CANDIDATES HELD A DEBATE.

...I WOULD JUST LIKE TO SAY THAT IF I AM ELECTED, I WOULD **NEVER** VOTE TO CUT SOCIAL SECURITY.

WELL, LET ME MAKE IT CLEAR THAT I WOULD **NEVER NEVER** VOTE TO CUT SOCIAL SECURITY.

BY CONTRAST, I WOULD **NEVER NEVER NEVER** VOTE TO CUT SOCIAL SECURITY.

IT WAS A LENGTHY DEBATE.

...I WOULD **NEVER NEVER NEVER NEVER**

SEVERAL DAYS BEFORE THE ELECTION BOB FOREHEAD'S CAMP GOT RESULTS OF A FINAL POLL.

HOW **DOES** IT LOOK?

NOT GOOD.

ELECTION DAY, 1982.
------7:20 A.M.
The FIRST VOTERS EMERGE From the POLLS in BOB FORE-HEAD'S *congressional* DISTRICT.

PARDON ME, MA'AM. I'M FROM NETWORK NEWS. WE'RE TAKING A VOTER SURVEY. WOULD YOU LIKE TO BE THE VOTER?

Well, O.K.

THANK YOU... *now*, IF YOU'LL JUST STEP *into* OUR MOBILE SURVEY *unit*...

WXXX
"MANIAC NEWS" MOBILE SURVEY UNIT

THE VAN WAS DIVIDED *into* MANY SMALL ROOMS. THE VOTER WAS LED *into* THE FIRST ONE.

ALL RIGHT NOW, WHOM DID YOU VOTE FOR FOR CONGRESS?

ALLEN SOUP.

WHY?

Well, FIRST OF ALL, *he* used to SIT *in* FRONT OF ME IN CHEMISTRY *class* IN HIGH SCHOOL *and* HE ALWAYS LET ME LOOK OVER HIS SHOULDER DURING *tests.* HE'S REALLY *very nice.*

AS SHE SPOKE, THE MAN ENTERED THE DATA *into* A COMPUTER TERMINAL!

HAVE YOU EVER VOTED FOR BOB FOREHEAD?

NO. AND I NEVER WOULD. HE'S *in* THE WRONG PARTY.

THE VOTER WAS CLASSI-FIED AS A HARD CORE SUPPORTER OF THE *challen-ger*, BUT QUES-TIONS REMAINED AS TO HOW THE CAMPAIGN HAD AFFECTED HER ON DEEPER LEVELS.

IN THE SECOND ROOM, SHE WAS *Examined* BY a tEAM OF PHYSICIANS *and* DIAGNOSED AS SUFFERING FROM CHARISMASTRENUOSIS, *a nervous condition* BELIEVED TO RESULT FROM WILLFULLY RESISTING CHARISMA.

BZZZT!

AH.

I WONDER HOW WE EVER GOT ALONG WITHOUT A HYDRO-ELEC-TRONIC TONGUE DEPRESSER.

DURING FOUR YEARS IN WASHINGTON, THERE WERE SEVERAL *museums* THAT GINGER FOREHEAD ALWAYS *intended* to VISIT, BUT NEVER DID.

HIGH ON HER LIST WAS THE *Renowned* FUBBLINGHORN, MUSEUM, FEATURING THE WORLD'S LARGEST *collection* OF RADIATOR PIPES, 1845 to THE PRESENT.

OOH! AH! GOLLY! Gee.

ONE NIGHT, *however*, AROUND 3:00 A.M., GINGER *came* WITH *inches* OF VISITING THE FUBBLINGHORN IN A CHEVY NOVA at 85 MILES *an* HOUR.

THE MILTON R. FUBBLINGHORN MUSEUM

SCREEEEECH

YOU ALMOST **KILLED** US!

I'VE GOT to LOSE THEM.

SAID THE *mussy-haired* MAN.

"...THEM" Being *two* POLICE CARS in hot PURSUIT.

POLICE

POLICE

WHY DON'T WE JUST STOP and EXPLAIN? AFTER ALL, I DIDN'T **MEAN** to BLOW UP THAT BANK. I THOUGHT THAT GADGET WAS AN AMPLIFIER FOR *your* RADIO...

...BY THE WAY, WHAT **IS** tHAt gadget Anyway?

NOT NOW, SHEILA.

IT WAS SOMETIME AFTER DAWN SOMEWHERE in VIRGINIA tHAt THEY FINALLY ELUDED tHEIR PURSUERS.

WHO **ARE** YOU, ANYWAY?

MY NAME IS...

UH,

...SLADE!

...I play tHE Guitar. I HOPE to RECORD SOMEDAY... I make MY BUCKS in tHE...uh..in the HARDWARE BUSINESS.

SAID THE MUSSY-HAIRED TYRANIAN DEFENSE MINISTER.

YOU PLAY tHE GUITAR?! REALLY?!!

...I...I do SOME SINGING. ...MOSTLY FOR MYSELF, BUT...

"SLADE" PULLED HIS GUITAR FROM tHE TRUNK and PLAYED A TUNE.

GINGER JOINED IN.

I LIKE YOUR VOICE. I BET WE COULD PUT SOMETHING TOGETHER.

THEY ROCKED and BOPPED FOR MOST OF tHAT DAY.

LATER, BOB FOREHEAD GOT A CALL FROM HIS WIFE.

...WHERE'D YOU GO LAST NIGHT?... ...to YOUR SISTER'S IN RICHMOND?

...AT **ONE** O'CLOCK in THE **MORNING**?!!
...

FOURTEEN *consecutive* HOURS...

COME ON, BABY, COME ON! **DAMN!** COME ON.

...PROBABLY the *longest* time HE'D *ever* SPENT DOING *any* ONE THING.

GLOM-MANIA

It all STARTED in THE MORNING WHEN *he'd* COME *in* to BUY a PAPER and HAPPENED to WANDER *into* THE *rear* OF THE STORE.

VIDEO ARCADE

HE'D *always* WONDERED WHAT THE APPEAL WAS ...OF VIDEO GAMES.

TWO HOURS *and* 23 DOLLARS *later*, HE *had* A PRETTY GOOD IDEA.

PROBABLY HE IDENTIFIED With tHE **LITTLE** MAN BEING CHASED THROUGH tHE MAZE BY tHE MAN-EATING VIDEO GAME WHICH tHREAtENED to DEVOUR HIM UNLESS HE FED IT WITH tHE QUARTERS HE FOUND *along* THE WAY.

25 · 25 · 25 · 25

BUT HE ALSO IDENTIFIED *with* tHE HUNGER,...tHE MiNDLESS, ENDLESS HUNGER *of* tHE MACHINE.

VIDEO ARCADE

...THAT. MACHINE MAKES A LOT OF SENSE.

SAID BOB FOREHEAD.

EO ARCADE

YES, I KNOW...

SAID tHE VIDEO GAME TRANSITION COUNSELOR.

..I'D ALMOST SAY IT'S MORE LOGICAL THAN MY LIFE...

YES, YES, BUT WE KNOW that's NOT TRUE...

WHY NOT? IT GOES TO MY VERY ESSENCE. I MEAN, WHAT **ELSE** IS THERE?

AS REQUIRED BY STATE LAW, the VIDEO GAME COUNSELOR WAS ON DUTY at the ARCADE to HELP INTENSIVE PLAYERS to INTEGRATE their VIDEO GAME EXPERIENCES WITH "REAL LIFE!"

VIDEO ARCADE

I'D LIKE TO LIVE HERE.

COME NOW... YOU'RE NOT BEING REALISTIC.

YES, I AM.

NO, NO. ...YOU SEE, THESE ARE MERELY GAMES...

NO! THEY'RE **ALIVE!**

IT TOOK A WHILE, BUT EVENTUALLY BOB GOT REORIENTED and WENT HOME.

NEWSPAPERS MAGAZINE VIDEO ARCADE   RESTA

MEANWHILE, HIS WIFE, GINGER, WAS ORIENTING HERSELF TOWARD A POSSIBLE SINGING CAREER.

GIMME GIMME GIMME
GIMME GIMME GIMME
GIMME ♪
GIMME ♪...

SANG GINGER FOREHEAD in that afternoon AUDITION.

THE SONG, "GIMME, GIMME, GIMME," WAS WRITTEN BY the MUSSY-HAIRED MAN.

I LIKE IT. YOU GOT ENERGY. I'LL GIVE YOU A SHOT ... NEXT TUESDAY.

SAID the OWNER OF "DANNY'S PLACE" in NORTHERN VIRGINIA.

GINGER WAS ECSTATIC.

Danny's PLACE
Danny's PLACE
LIVE MUSIC
ROCK BANDS

I CAN HARDLY BELIEVE IT! OUR FIRST GIG!

YEH... and GUESS WHAT...

...I WROTE A NEW SONG. IT'S CALLED : "I WANTCHA, WANTCHA, WANTCHA!" YOU COULD LEARN IT TONIGHT!

NOT TONIGHT, SLADE.

WHY NOT?

I JUST CAN'T.

SHEILA, WHY WON'T YOU TELL ME WHERE YOU LIVE?

WHY WON'T **YOU** TELL ME WHAT THAT GADGET WAS THAT BLEW UP THE BANK?

I WILL. I WILL. NOT NOW.

...FORGET IT.

GINGER GOT BACK in TIME to SHOWER and CHANGE BEFORE HER husband GOT HOME.

YOU READY?

ALL SET.

SINCE HIS FIRST TERM in CONGRESS, BOB and GINGER HAD NEVER FAILED to ATTEND THE ANNUAL "TOXIC WASTE BALL" AS GUESTS OF THE OXBOGGLES.

NORMALLY, BOB enjoyed THIS AFFAIR. ⋈ THIS YEAR HE SEEMED RESTLESS.

AFTER the PRESENTATION OF tHE "DUMPER OF THE YEAR" AWARD, BOB STOOD UP.

LET'S GO.

HE DROVE AN UNUSUAL ROUTE HOME!

I WANT TO MAKE ONE QUICK STOP.

LATER:

BOB, YOU SAID JUST ONE GAME. WE'VE BEEN HERE FOR 3 HOURS!

JUST ONE MORE. JUST ONE MORE.

VIDEO ARCADE

GLOM-MANIA

ONE PERSON WHO DIDN'T NEED TO BE SOLD ON THE **V-16** WAS COLONEL ANNOYU, THE RULER OF TYRANIA.

I want THE **V-16**. **LOTS** OF THEM! ...20...30... **40**... **LOTS** OF THEM!

I'LL **TRY**, BOSS, BUT IT HAS TO BE APPROVED BY CONGRESS.

said HIS MUSSY-HAIRED DEFENSE MINISTER FROM WASHINGTON.

WELL, GET TO WORK!

WHO WAS THAT?

asked GINGER FOREHEAD, entering THE ROOM.

HUH? OH...NOBODY. ...UH, LET'S REHEARSE.

AS THEY REHEARSED, THE MUSSY-HAIRED MAN TRIED TO REMEMBER ALL THE CONGRESSMEN HE KNEW,

...*and* GINGER TRIED TO FORGET.

EVERY MORNING EDGAR BULCHENFORTEN FILLS A CANVAS BAG WITH SOME OF THE MOST IMPORTANT PEOPLE in WASH-ING-TON.

The Daily ACCESS

THEN HE HOPS ON HIS BIKE and RIDES ALL OVER TOWN DELIVERING THEM to VARIOUS OFFICES and RESTAURANTS.

RIGHT ON TIME!

SWISH!

The Daily ACCESS

(HE HAS A POWERFUL SIDEARM DELIVERY.)

WELL, THAT'S NOT EXACTLY HOW HE WORKS, ...BUT ALMOST.

MY GOVERNMENT WANTS TO BUY SOME V-16 FIGHTER PLANES. WE'LL NEED CONGRESSIONAL APPROVAL. I'M TOLD YOU'RE WELL-CONNECTED.

SAID THE MUSSY-HAIRED DEFENSE MINISTER OF TYRANIA

MR. BULCHENFORTEN BEGAN to OUTLINE A STRATEGY.

...OH, BY THE WAY, I'm ATTENDING A COCKTAIL PARTY at 6 O'CLOCK. YOU'D DO WELL to JOIN ME.

Fine, BUT I'LL ONLY HAVE an HOUR.

AMONG THOSE PRESENT at THE COCKTAIL PARTY WAS *Congressman* CHARLES BLURWELL, CHAIRMAN OF tHE POWERFUL HOUSE MISCELLANY *committee.*

BLURWELL WIELDS A LOT OF INFLUENCE. I'LL *introduce* YOU.

LATER:

ANOTHER PERSON YOU SHOULD MEET IS **THAT** FELLOW:

...BOB FOREHEAD. HE'S THE LEADER OF tHE JFK-LOOK-ALIKE CAUCUS. THAT'S 19 VOTES.

ANOTHER TIME! I HAVE TO GO NOW.

AFTER THE MUSSY-HAIRED MAN LEFT, EDGAR CHATTED BRIEFLY WITH CONGRESSMAN FOREHEAD.

...HOW'S YOUR WIFE?

OH...UH, FINE.

HOW BOB'S WIFE **ACTUALLY** WAS WAS VERY NERVOUS.

BUT BOB DIDN'T KNOW THAT.

WHAT IF I LOSE MY VOICE OR FORGET THE LYRICS?!

SHE CHANGED *into* HER SECRET OUTFIT *and* HURRIED *to* MEET A *certain* MUSSY-HAIRED GUITARIST.

RELAX, SHEILA. YOU'LL BE GREAT!

And, IN FACT, SHE WAS.

GIMME GIMME GIMME GIMME GIMME GIMME GIMME GIMME...

...AND SHE REMEMBERED ALL THE LYRICS.

HE GRIPPED THE *heartstrings* OF THE NATION, THIS CREATURE FROM OUTER SPACE KNOWN AS: "**E.M.** THE EXTRAORDINARILY-MERCHANDISABLE".

E.M.

WITHIN *months* OF HIS *cinematic* DEBUT, *hundreds* OF PRODUCTS BORE *his* LIKENESS, ...*and* SOLD LIKE *crazy!*

EM

BUT NOT EVERYONE WAS SWEPT UP *in* THE **E.M.** CRAZE.

...UH, W-WHAT IS IT?

asked BOB FOREHEAD UPON OPENING HIS CHRISTMAS GIFT FROM HIS WIFE.

IT'S *an* **E.M.** ELECTRIC SHAVER.

BZZZ

EM

WHAT'S "E.M."?

DON'T YOU REMEMBER? ...THAT MOVIE WE SAW LAST *month*?

WHAT MOVIE?

SUDDENLY, GINGER RECALLED *that* IT WASN'T BOB WITH WHOM SHE HAD SEEN THAT MOVIE, BUT RATHER

ANOTHER FELLOW

...WITH MUSSY HAIR.

SHE DROPPED THE SUBJECT *and* OPENED HER GIFT FROM BOB. IT WAS A SCARF. IT WAS AWFUL. HE HAD SUCH BAD TASTE.

UH, THANK YOU. IT'S ...UH...UH, THANK YOU.

THIS CHRISTMAS RECESS WAS THE FIRST TIME in A LONG TIME that THEY'D SPENT any TIME TOGETHER. THEIR *communication* WASN'T GREAT.

WHO **IS** THIS PERSON?!

AM I REALLY MARRIED TO HIM?!

I'VE GOT TO WORK ON MY BACK-HAND.

Meanwhile, THE MUSSY-HAIRED MAN WAS A GREAT GUITARIST, *and* HE APPRECIATED HER SINGING.

WHAT MORE COULD SHE WANT IN A MAN?

I DON'T KNOW WHAT IT IS THAT KEEPS ME WITH BOB.

CONFIDED GINGER TO HER BEST FRIEND.

... MAYBE IT'S FORCE-OF-HABIT. MAYBE FORCE-OF-HABIT IS STRONGER THAN LOVE.

OH, DARLING, I'VE FALLEN IN FORCE-OF-HABIT WITH YOU.

and I WITH YOU.

BOB *and* GINGER MIGHT SAY *to* EACH OTHER *in the* MOVIE VERSION OF THEIR LIVES.

BUT *the* REAL-LIFE VERSION OF THEIR LIVES *is* CONSIDERABLY LESS ARTICULATED.

?!

I'M GOING OVER TO THE GYM.

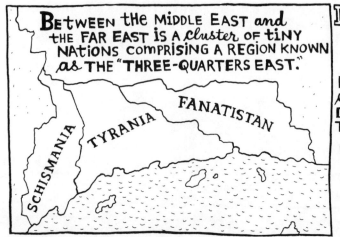

BETWEEN the MIDDLE EAST and the FAR EAST is a *cluster* OF tiny NATIONS COMPRISING A REGION KNOWN *as* THE "THREE-QUARTERS EAST."

SCHISMANIA

TYRANIA

FANATISTAN

DESPITE ITS SMALL SIZE, tHIS REGION *contains* DISPROPORTIONATELY LARGE DEPOSITS OF A VARIETY OF RAW *materials.*

NOTABLE AMONG tHESE:
THE THREE-QUARTERS EAST PRODUCES *the* RAW MATERIALS FOR **44%** OF *the* WORLD'S ARTIFICIAL FOOD ADDITIVES.

HERE WE see two TYRANIAN additive miners at work.

TYRANIA, **THE** LARGEST ADDITIVE PRODUCER *in* tHE REGION, IS RULED BY *the* MILITARY GOVERNMENT OF COLONEL ARRESTES TORTURO ANNOYU.

WE'VE GOT TO TAKE BACK THAT TERRITORY. IT'S **OURS!**

THE territory HE'S REFERRING TO IS PRESENTLY *under* tHE CONTROL OF FANATISTAN *and* HAS BEEN FOR 15 YEARS. IT IS *considered to* BE RICH *in* CERTAIN *valuable* MINERALS.

THE TWO *countries* HAVE FOUGHT TO A *StaLeMate* OVER tHIS TERRITORY FOR YEARS.

THOSE V-16 FIGHTER PLANES COULD MAKE tHE DIFFERENCE!

I'M WORKING ON IT, BOSS... THESE THINGS TAKE TIME!

SAID tHE *mussy*-HAIRED TYRANIAN DEFENSE MINISTER *from* WASHINGTON.

ANOTHER THING THAT TAKES TIME IS REHEARSING *a* ROCK 'N' ROLL ACT.

...*Let's* GO tHROUGH it *once* MORE. THERE'S GOING *to* BE AN IMPORTANT GUY FROM tHE MUSIC BUSINESS *in* tHE AUDIENCE TONIGHT.

O.K.

BUT SOMETIMES HARD WORK PAYS OFF. THAT NIGHT IT APPEARED TO.

I LIKE YOUR ACT! REALLY! IT'S HOT! HOW'D YOU LIKE TO MAKE A RECORD?

COME ON, JOE. GET THIS SPARE and WE'RE BACK in the GAME.

BOWLING SHOE RENTAL

NORMALLY JOE WOULD HAVE HAD NO TROUBLE.

BUT TONIGHT HE WASN'T HIS USUAL SELF.

@#%&!!

JOE, RELAX! ...RELAX!

SAID HIS TEAMMATE RALPH.

BUT HE COULDN'T.

I DON'T KNOW WHAT'S WRONG.

BUT HE DID KNOW.

LATER, AFTER the GAME, and SEVERAL BEERS, IT CAME OUT. HIS EYES BECAME MISTY AS HE SPOKE.

ALL my LIFE... SINCE I WAS NINE, I'VE HAD A DREAM. ...I'VE... I'VE WANTED... TO RAISE WILD YAKS. ...SINCE the FIRST TIME I EVER SAW ONE that DAY AT the ZOO...THEY'RE **BEAUTIFUL** ANIMALS!...

BUT THEY'RE ALSO EXPENSIVE... **VERY** EXPENSIVE...and I'D WANT TO OWN A HERD OF THEM. THAT'S THE ONLY PROPER WAY TO DO IT. and THEN I'D HAVE TO BUY LAND, **LOTS** OF LAND... and YAK FOOD...

I THOUGHT WHEN I GOT TRANSFERRED TO MY NEW JOB, I'D BE MAKING ENOUGH TO BUY ONE OR TWO YAKS A YEAR,... BUT THEN MY CAR BROKE DOWN and MY KID STARTED COLLEGE, and...

I DIDN'T KNOW YOU'D BEEN TRANSFERRED! ...TO WHAT DIVISION?

RALPH and JOE WORKED FOR THE GLOMINOID CORPORATION.

THE WEAPONS DIVISION. IT'S A SECRET PROJECT.

A JOLT OF ADRENALIN SHOT THROUGH RALPH.

IS IT...

...IS IT THE CREDIT CARD BOMB PROJECT?

AFTER 6 BEERS JOE WAS NOT VERY SECRETIVE. **YEP.**

LISTEN, JOE, I THINK I CAN HELP YOU. IF YOU COULD GET ME ACCESS TO THAT BOMB, I KNOW A GUY WHO WOULD PAY US A LOT OF MONEY... A **LOT** OF MONEY...

...I'M TALKING ABOUT A **LOT** OF WILD YAKS!

JOE STARED INTO HIS BEER MUG. THERE WAS A DREAMY LOOK IN HIS EYES.

TO GO TO SCHOOL. I'm STUDYING FOR MY M.B.A. WHEN I GRADUATE, I WILL RETURN TO my PEOPLE and HELP them BRIDGE the GAP BETWEEN OUR TRIBAL HERITAGE and the AGE OF HIGH TECHNOLOGY.

TRAFFIC WAS SLOW-MOVING. THEY TALKED FOR QUITE A WHILE!

THE MORE GINGER LEARNED ABOUT THE GAZUBI TRIBE the MORE INTRIGUED SHE BECAME, ...and the ANGRIER SHE FELT TOWARD COLONEL ANNOYU.

IN THE DAYS that FOLLOWED, SHE FOUND HERSELF thinking RECURRINGLY ABOUT the CONVERSATION WITH THE CAB DRIVER.

BUT THEN SHE GOT CAUGHT UP in THE EXCITEMENT OF RECORDING HER FIRST RECORD.

I CAN HARDLY BELIEVE IT!

AT the SAME time, A MAN NAMED JOE COULD HARDLY BELIEVE THAT **HIS** DREAM OF OWNING A HERD OF WILD YAKS WAS WITHIN HIS GRASP.

I...I'LL DO IT... I'LL TRY TO GET YOU THE BOMB...

HE BEGAN to FEEL IT ON HiS WAY *to* WORK,

A ...SLOWLY EMER-GING ANXIETY.

A SHORT WHILE LATER, *in* THE LOCKER-ROOM, AS HE CHANGED *INTO* HIS PROTECTIVE SUIT, HIS ANXIETY BECAME FEAR. HE BEGAN TO IMAGINE HIMSELF *in* PRISON!

RULES LIST 7K
NO. SG-8AZ
CODE DIVISION
B 7J EMPLOYEE
MUST CARRY C
7KJ-19 PASS T
GAIN ENTRY T
SECTION 5-J-F
ANY EMPLOY
SEEKING TO A
A CODE X-5 A
WITHOUT A C
10-WX PASS
MUST BE AU
RIZED BY SU
ER IN CODE

FOR A **moment**, HE PAN-ICKED.

But *then* ANOTHER IMAGE CAME TO MIND... AN IMAGE OF A MOUNTAIN RANGE, INHAB-ITED BY A HERD OF *the* MOST BEAUTIFUL *animals* HE'D EVER SEEN,... WILD YAKS.

I'VE GOT TO TAKE *the* RISK!

ACTUALLY, HIS CHANCES OF GETTING AWAY *with* IT WERE PROBABLY QUITE GOOD. HE WAS WELL-REGARDED, ...*and* TRUSTED.

IN *the* DISHWASHER DIVISION, JOE'S IDEAS *and* SUGGESTIONS HAD INSPIRED SEVERAL MAJOR INNOVATIONS *in* DISHWASHING TECHNOLOGY.

THE GLOMINOID CORPORATION HOPED HE WOULD BE EQUALLY HELPFUL IN THEIR WEAPONS DIVISION in THE PERFECTION OF THEIR NEW BOMB THAT WOULD **KILL** ONLY THOSE PEOPLE WHO DON'T CARRY CREDIT CARDS.

I'LL CLOSE UP FOR YOU, JOHN. YOU LOOK TIRED.

THANKS, JOE! I 'PRECIATE IT!

JOE ACTED FAST.

TESTING AREA K-74

RESTRICTED AREA

HE LOADED SEVERAL CRITICAL MATERIALS INTO HIS LUNCH BOX, and TOOK THEM HOME.

RESTRICTED AREA KRD-7J SEC. 5J-Z17G

THAT NIGHT HE TOLD RALPH OF HIS PROGRESS.

THAT'S GREAT!

THEN RALPH TRIED TO TELEPHONE THE MUSSY-HAIRED MAN.

...BUT THE LINE WAS BUSY.

YES, OF **COURSE**, WE'RE GLAD WE MADE THE RECORD, BUT YOU'RE SUPPOSED TO BE **PROMOTING** IT! IT'S NOT ON THE RADIO! IT'S NOT IN THE STORES! ...**DO** SOMETHING!...

MEANWHILE, ON CAPITOL HILL, OPPOSITION WAS MOUNTING AGAINST A PROPOSED **SALE** OF V-16 FIGHTER PLANES *to* TYRANIA.

...COLONEL ANNOYU HAS A SHAMEFUL RECORD *in* THE AREA OF HUMAN RIGHTS!

THE HOUSE MISCELLANY COMMITTEE DECIDED TO TAKE ACTION.

I PROPOSE THAT WE SEND A DELEGATION ON A FACT-FINDING MISSION TO TYRANIA.

AMONG THE MEMBERS OF THE PROPOSED DELEGATION WAS CONGRESSMAN BOB FOREHEAD.

HE TOLD HIS WIFE ABOUT THE TRIP.

"TYRANIA"?!... UM, CAN I COME WITH YOU?

UH, O.K.

SAID BOB ON HIS WAY TO WORK.

THE HEARING ROOM WAS BUZZING WITH TENSION **AS** CONGRESSMAN BOB FOREHEAD *entered* AND HURRIED *to* HIS SEAT.

THE SUBJECT OF these HEARINGS WAS A SCANDAL that HAD DEVELOPED in the the **I.P.A.**, OR: "**INFLUENCE PROTECTION AGENCY**." THE FIRST WITNESS WAS A SPOKESMAN FOR the *administration*.

IN RECENT WEEKS, MR. CHAIRMAN, THERE HAVE BEEN A NUMBER OF SCURRILOUS ATTACKS ON the I.P.A., PARTICULARLY WITH REGARD TO ITS USE OF PAPER SHREDDERS in the CLEAN-UP AND REMOVAL OF HAZARDOUS INFORMATION...

I WANT TO TAKE this OPPORTUNITY TO STRESS THE IMPORTANCE OF THIS CLEAN-UP PROGRAM...

THE DAILY OPERATION OF OUR GOVERNMENT IS DEPENDENT ON A COMPLEX NETWORK OF CHANNELS OF INFLUENCE. ANY SIGNIFICANT LEAKAGE OF HAZARDOUS INFORMATION into THE MEDIA OR THE HANDS OF ENVIRONMENTALISTS COULD CAUSE SERIOUS, IF NOT IRREPARABLE, DAMAGE TO THIS VITAL NETWORK,...

...AND POSSIBLY A BREAKDOWN OF THE ENTIRE INFLUENCOLOGICAL SYSTEM.

A CHILL PASSED THROUGH CONGRESSMAN FOREHEAD AS HE LISTENED.

IT IS INTERESTING TO NOTE THAT MANY OPPONENTS OF THIS PROGRAM ARE THOSE WHO PROMOTE **BIG SPENDING** BY GOVERNMENT. THEIR MOTIVES ARE CLEARLY POLITICAL...

...FOR HERE, IN "SUPERFUN," WE HAVE A **LUNCH PROGRAM** FUNDED ENTIRELY BY PRIVATE INDUSTRY, PROVIDING IRREFUTABLE EVIDENCE THAT **VOLUNTEERISM** COULD WORK IF ONLY WE LET IT!

THE TESTIMONY HAD A POWERFUL IMPACT ON BOB FOREHEAD,

...WHICH HE DISCUSSED OVER LUNCH WITH MR. OX-BOGGLE.

OUR SPEECH-SEEKING MISSILE IS THE MOST INTELLIGENT EXPLOSIVE DEVICE in the WORLD. SEVERAL OF THESE MISSILES HAVE EARNED Ph.D.'s FROM STANFORD. ANOTHER WAS OFFERED A PROFESSORSHIP AT M.I.T.

THIS WAS THE 14th DEFENSE SUBCONTRACTOR TO VISIT CONGRESSMAN FOREHEAD THAT DAY.

...THE PROPOSED SALE OF V-16 FIGHTER PLANES to TYRANIA WOULD ENABLE US TO LOWER THE PRICE OF THESE ATTACHED MISSILES FROM 78.5 MILLION TO 78.3 MILLION DOLLARS A PIECE.

THE MAN LEFT HIS CARD.

KILTEK CORPORATION

"KILL MORE FOR LESS"

STEVEN PELF
WASHINGTON
REPRESENTATIVE

LEAVING HIS OFFICE at THE END OF THE DAY, BOB HAD tHAT LOBBIED LOOK.

THE NEXT DAY BOB and HIS WIFE FLEW TO TYRANIA WITH THE U.S. CONGRESSIONAL DELEGATION.

THEY WERE GIVEN A SPECTACULAR WELCOME...

...THEN DRIVEN DOWN THE HIGHWAY TO THE GOVERNMENT PALACE.

QUIK LIK♥

FROZEN CUSTARD

ITCHCO AUTO SEAT COVERS

AUTO PARTS

CHICKEN MACHE OPEN

BURGER KONG

PIZZA HOUSE

WOODEN WAFFLES

NAN'S HOUSE

SH

LATER AT A RECEPTION:

CONGRESSMAN FOREHEAD, I'D LIKE TO INTRODUCE YOU AND YOUR WIFE TO THE DEFENSE MINISTER OF TYRANIA...

GINGER FOREHEAD LOOKED DOWN at the FLOOR AS SHE SHOOK HANDS WITH TYRANIA'S DEFENSE minister at A RECEPTION in TYRANIA.

I HOPE HE DOESN'T RECOGNIZE ME.

SHE NEEDN'T have WORRIED, HOWEVER, BECAUSE THE DEFENSE MINISTER HARDLY LOOKED AT HER. HIS MIND WAS ON SOMEONE ELSE, FAR AWAY...

...OR SO HE THOUGHT.

GINGER WAS in SHOCK.

"..."DEFENSE"?! MINISTER"?! ...I DON'T BELIEVE IT! ...SO THAT'S WHAT HE MEANT WHEN HE TOLD ME HE WAS in the HARDWARE BUSINESS!..

THE NEXT DAY COLONEL ANNOYU took the congressional DELEGATION on A tour OF THE TYRANIAN CAPITAL. THE FIRST stop WAS the SHOPPING MALL.

YOU'LL NOTICE THE SHOPPERS FREELY EXERCISING THEIR HUMAN RIGHT TO BUY AMERICAN GOODS.

SOCK CITY

IN one STORE, CONGRESSMAN FOREHEAD NOTICED A HUGE DISPLAY OF CORN PADS that HAD BEEN MANUFACTURED in HIS DISTRICT.

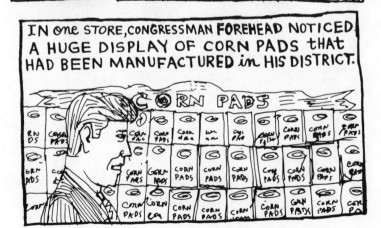

CORN PADS

IT REMINDED HIM OF A MEETING HE'D HAD RECENTLY WITH A REPRESENTATIVE OF "THE FEDERATION OF AMERICAN CORN PAD DISTRIBUTORS."

...IF THE U.S. FAILS TO SELL V-16 FIGHTER PLANES TO TYRANIA, THAT NATION MIGHT TURN TO THE SOVIET UNION FOR THEIR WEAPONS.

...IT **STARTS** WITH WEAPONS. THE NEXT THING YOU KNOW, THEY'LL BE BUYING SOVIET-MADE CORN PADS!

THAT NIGHT BOB FOREHEAD GOT A LONG DISTANCE CALL FROM MR. OXBOGGLE in AMERICA.

THE DUMPING RIGHTS ACT IS IN TROUBLE. THIS IS A BAD TIME FOR YOU TO BE AWAY.

IT SURELY WAS. BOB WAS MISSING A LOT. FOR SOME PEOPLE in WASHINGTON, BUSINESS WAS BOOMING.

SCANDAL DYNAMICS INC.

"SCANDAL DYNAMICS." GOOD MORNING...

...YES SIR, WE PROVIDE CAREER COUNSELING FOR MAXIMUM UTILIZATION OF THE CIRCUMSTANCES OF SCANDAL... YES SIR, WE DO HANDLE BOOKS AND FILMS... YESSIR ...

THE DARK PICTURE MR. OXBOGGLE PAINTED OF THE EROSION OF HUMAN RIGHTS *in* AMERICA CAUSED BOB FORE-HEAD TO VIEW TYRANIA WITH MORE TOLERANCE.

WHY DON'T WE LET THEM BUY THOSE FIGHTER PLANES?...

THEY SEEM LIKE NICE ENOUGH FOLKS.

MAYBE SO.

THAT NIGHT BOB DREAMED ABOUT LOBBYISTS, OCEANS OF LOBBYISTS.

GINGER DIDN'T DREAM AT ALL. SHE COULDN'T SLEEP. FINALLY SHE GOT UP *and* WENT FOR A WALK.

AT THE END OF A PALACE HALL-WAY SHE HAPPENED UPON THE DEFENSE MINISTER'S OFFICE. THE DOOR WAS OPEN. SHE WALKED *in*.

A FEW MINUTES LATER SHE HEARD VOICES *and* FOOTSTEPS. SHE DUCKED BEHIND A COUCH.

SO WHEN DO WE GET THE BOMB?

SAID COLONEL ANNOYU TO HIS DEFENSE MINISTER.

WE'VE **GOT** IT.

MY CONTACT FROM THE KILTEK CORPORATION HOOKED IT UP TO A SPEECH-SEEKING MISSILE. HE INSTALLED THE ENTIRE UNIT ON ONE OF OUR BOMBERS. IT'S AT THE AIRPORT, ALL SET TO GO.

EXCELLENT! ...THOSE GAZUBIS WON'T KNOW WHAT HIT THEM!

"GAZUBIS"?!!

THOUGHT GINGER FOREHEAD, HIDING BEHIND THE COUCH.

HAVING RECENTLY MADE FRIENDS WITH A GAZUBI and TAKEN an INTEREST in THEIR CULTURE,

SHE WAS EVEN TRYING TO LEARN THEIR LANGUAGE!

I WANT TO DROP THE BOMB AS SOON AS POSSIBLE. IT SHOULD WIPE OUT THE WHOLE TRIBE!

At THAT POINt, THE DEFENSE MINISTER UTTERED TWO SYLLABLES, DESTINED TO IMPACT NEGATIVELY ON HIS PERSONAL LIFE:

O.K.

"**O.K**"?!!...

SHRIEKED GINGER, LEAPING INTO VIEW.

...THAT'S "O.K." WITH YOU, HUH?!!

SHE SHOUTED, DIVING AT HIM LIKE A RABID WILDCAT.

WHAA?

I THOUGHT YOU WERE A SENSITIVE MUSICIAN, YOU LOUSY CREEP! YOU PHONY RAT! YOU CRUMMY JERK!

POW!

OW!

GUARDS! GUARDS!

TWO SOLDIERS RUSHED IN AND PULLED GINGER AWAY.

...YOU SNAKE! YOU MONSTER! YOU...

SH-SHEILA?

OH NO!

DO YOU KNOW WHO THIS LADY IS?

SHE... SHE'S ...A SINGER.

NO! SHE'S CONGRESSMAN FOREHEAD'S WIFE!...

...AND SHE KNOWS, TOO MUCH! WE CAN'T LET HER GO. SHE'S GOING TO HAVE TO HAVE AN "ACCIDENT."

BUT FIRST THINGS FIRST. YOU KEEP HER GUARDED. I'M GOING TO THE AIRPORT. BEFORE ANYTHING ELSE GOES WRONG, ...

...WE'VE GOT TO DROP THAT BOMB NOW!

As COLONEL ANNOYU HEADED FOR THE AIRPORT, *intent* ON BOMBING THE GAZUBI TRIBE INTO EXTINCTION,...

CAN'T YOU DRIVE ANY FASTER?!

... GINGER FOREHEAD FOUND HERSELF HELD PRISONER *in* THE OFFICE OF THE TYRANIAN DEFENSE MINISTER, WHO HAD THERETOFORE BEEN HER GUITARIST.

I'M SORRY, SHEILA, BUT I'VE GOT A JOB TO DO.

As SHE STOOD THERE IN THE GRIPS OF TWO PALACE GUARDS, GINGER'S EYES DARTED *around* THE ROOM, SEARCHING FOR A MEANS OF ESCAPE.

SUDDENLY, SHE CAUGHT SIGHT OF A FAMILIAR OBJECT ACROSS THE ROOM. IT WAS A TAPE CASSETTE PLAYER WITH A *certain* ATTACHED GADGET.

SLADE, WOULD YOU PLEASE ASK THESE BRUTES TO LET GO OF ME. AFTER ALL, THE DOOR IS LOCKED. THERE'S NO WAY I CAN ESCAPE.

UH ...O.K... LET GO OF HER, MEN.

GINGER SAT STILL FOR *several* MINUTES TO ALLAY SUSPICION.

THEN, *suddenly,* SHE BOLTED ACROSS THE ROOM, GRABBED THE CASSETTE PLAYER, *and* POINTED THE ATTACHED GADGET *at* HER CAPTORS.

SHEILA, NO!! PUT THAT DOWN!!

THE "GADGET" WAS A HIGH TECHNOLOGY WEAPON, KNOWN AS A **"CRAMM"** (CLOSE-RANGE AUTOMATIC MESS-MAKER).

DO AS I SAY, SLADE, OR I'LL BLOW YOUR BRAINS OUT! I KNOW HOW TO USE THIS THING. REMEMBER?

UH...Y-YES... UH...ANYTHING YOU S-SAY!...

GET US A CAR and DRIVE ME TO THE AIRPORT. **FAST!**

OF C-COURSE! R-RIGHT AWAY!

IT WAS DAWN WHEN THEY REACHED THE AIRPORT. AT the END OF THE RUNWAY, A BOMBER, EQUIPPED WITH A SPEECH-SEEKING MISSILE, WAS TAKING OFF.

GET US A PLANE, SLADE.

UH... S-SURE.

A SHORT WHILE LATER THE DEFense Minister WAS AT the controls OF A TYRANIAN AIR FORCE CARGO PLANE

FOLLOW THAT BOMBER!

MEanwhile, ON A PLATEAU HIGH in the GAZU MOUNTAINS, there WAS MUCH ACTIVITY AS THE GAZUBI PEOPLE moved ABOUT in THE LIGHT OF THE NEW DAY...

AZU, GONGZAZA BUNGZUZU.

ZUNGZAZU BOZAGZU UNGZA BUNGZI.

GUNGUNGZA-BAZI ZONGZI, ZAZA.

...UNAWARE tHAT tHEIR IDLE CHATTER WAS ABOUT TO BE DETECTED BY tHE SENSING DEVICE in A SPEECH-SEEKING MISSILE.

WHEN DO WE FIRE THE MISSILE?

ANY MINUTE...

WE'RE *in* FIRING RANGE, SIR. YOU CAN GIVE THE ORDER ANY TIME...

FIRE!

SHOUTED COLONEL ANNOYU *moments* LATER,

...*and* A SPEECH-SEEKING MISSILE WAS LAUNCHED FROM THE BOMBER, ITS LANGUAGE-SENSING DEVICE GUIDING IT TOWARD *the*

MOUNTAIN PLATEAU, *twenty* MILES AWAY, WHERE THE GAZUBI LANGUAGE WAS BEING SPOKEN.

GUNGUNGZA, ZANG ZAZU. GANGZOW ZAZ?

GAGAZA ZOMZAZI GUMZAN GUZUZ.

FROM A CARGO PLANE 400 FEET ABOVE THE BOMBER, GINGER FOREHEAD WAS WATCHING.

WHEN SHE SAW THE MISSILE *in* FLIGHT, SHE RAN to THE HATCH OF THE PLANE.

THIS HAS **GOT** TO WORK!

SHE PULLED OUT A LANGUAGE STUDY CASSETTE SHE HAD BEEN USING TO LEARN THE GAZUBI LANGUAGE *and* INSERTED IT *into* THE TAPE CASSETTE PLAYER.

THEN SHE TURNED tHE VOLUME TO FULL BLAST and THREW IT OUT OF THE PLANE.

...HELLO: **GUNGUNGZA.** HELLO: **GUNGUNGZA.** HOW ARE YOU?: **GUNGZAZA BUNGZAZI?**

SOMETHING'S WRONG!... SHOUTED COLONEL ANNOYU in THE BOMBER. **THE MISSILE IS TURNING! IT'S GOING THE WRONG WAY!**

THE MISSILE ZEROED in ON THE CASSETTE PLAYER...

GAZUNZI. PLEASE PASS THE YAK BUTTER: **ZONGZONGA BONGZAZU ZABUNGZU**

...and MADE A DIRECT HIT.

KABOOM!!

OH NO! SAID COLONEL ANNOYU in UTTER DISMAY

ONE MORNING GINGER FOREHEAD WAS LATE FOR BREAKFAST.

PARA-CHUTES MOVE SLOWLY...

...and HITCHHIKING TAKES TIME.

PARENZI...

WHERE'S YOUR WIFE?

said A FELLOW CONGRESSMAN to BOB FOREHEAD at the STATE BREAKFAST in the TYRANIAN GOVERNMENT PALACE.

I'M NOT SURE. SHE'S SORT OF... independent.

WHEN GINGER FINALLY GOT BACK, BOB DISCOVERED SHE WAS more INDEPENDENT THAN HE'D THOUGHT.

You can't ALLOW the SALE OF FIGHTER PLANES to TYRANIA. COLONEL ANNOYU IS A MONSTER!

GINGER, YOU DON'T understand...

GINGER TOLD BOB A LITTLE BIT ABOUT Colonel ANNOYU'S EFFORT to WIPE out THE GAZUBI TRIBE.

Sometimes, GINGER, IT IS necessary TO tolerate the SUFFERING OF A FEW FOR a LARGER GOOD.

YOU PROBABLY DON'T KNOW THAT TYRANIA IS THE WORLD'S LARGEST PRODUCER OF "KABLAMMIUM ZILCHITE", A RARE STRATEGIC mineral NECESSARY in the manufacturing OF the EARTH-ENDER MISSILE.

FOR THIS REASON, IT IS IMPERATIVE THAT WE DEVELOP NEW COMPUTERS CAPABLE OF THINKING ABOUT IT FOR US, CAPABLE OF MAKING tHE TOUGH DECISION OF WHEN TO LAUNCH A NUCLEAR ATTACK...

SUDDENLY, GINGER FOREHEAD HAD A LOT TO THINK ABOUT.